Stoning sullen mask
fear not death,
that which abodes
within this Tomb
is not an ending...

it is an embryo.

Meaning and Relatedness

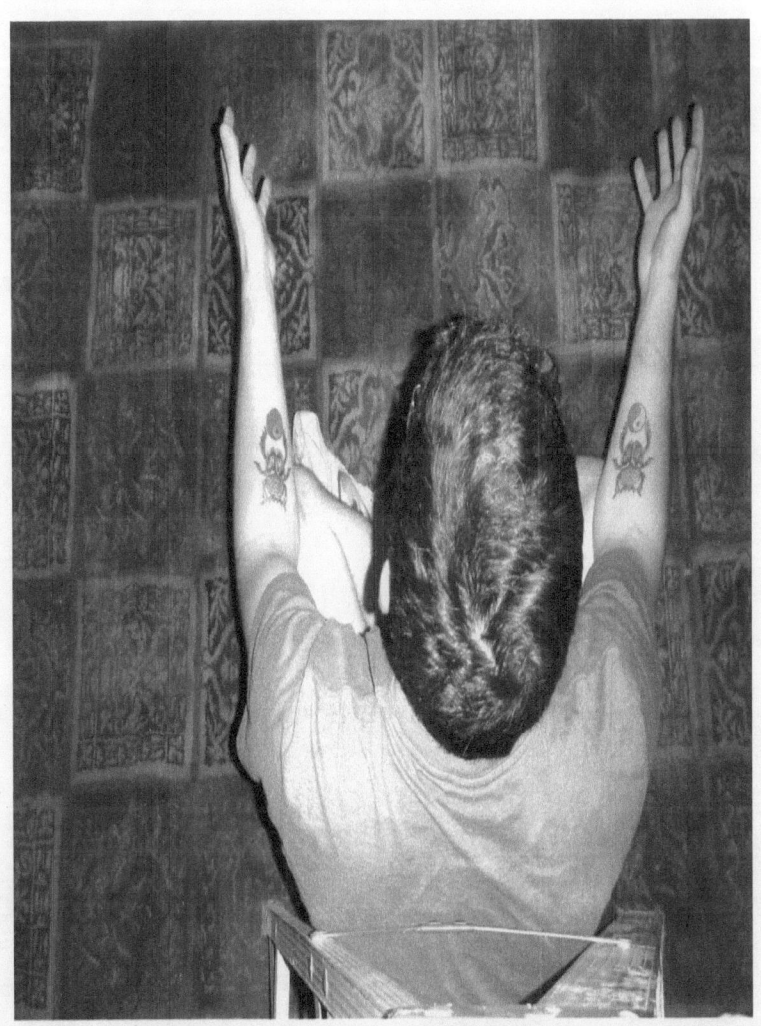

**Cover Photo of Meaning and Relatedness, First
Edition**

Meaning and Relatedness

Meaning and Relatedness

The Unleashed obscurity risen within Prison's own Prism

By   Khepri Rising

M A R

Book I of the Marah

All rights reserved by
Khepri Rising Enterprises
Published in X Isle
Copyright 2008
ISBN # 978-0-615-25547-7

2nd edition 2010

The original front cover photo shone on page 3 was taken by *my own Sun*, Kevin.

Beadle Scat

Dedicated to:

my Dad,

for the love and the caring that you have shone on me throughout the entirety of my life, with a unique and persistent selfless zeal.

With deep gratitude to:

*my dear friend **Trisha**,*

without whom this book would not have been possible.

Meaning and Relatedness

Part I.

the Embryo

Meaning and Relatedness

Slovenia's Solemn Slumber,
Salaam Shalom, Shoah, then...

I let her die with the waves, and as the Sun rolled downward over them, it was dark, without her, *and new*. My dreams have abandoned me again in this mundane desert… this sterile void. Caught in the midst of the morning's mourning and the tanned haziness of the coffee and dry creamer's swirls swirling; the haze rained rays from my still smudged glasses tarries me about and my spirit races before me to catch beams from dreams passing-past *fast* still-ly uncoiled and un-reconciled. I retreat to their comfort; even so it leaves me dazed, alone, and somehow inept to fathom this deep meaning and place of all places. My head hurt; I was hung over from life, and as I walked, breathing in the colors of autumn's fresh cooling chill, my *starry soul* felt all at once parched.

> The *Sun* is possibilities on the water,
> yet the womb soft and surrendering
> reveals a lucidity which falls-to, like
> pretty pink petals parted and the past flashes
> back crisp waking life: *as meanings past*.

Warm by the water, the Sun shows radiating brilliant yellow, rays warm, that seem to buzz with this life buzzing being-ness. *And sound…silent sound echoes the possibilities… 'what we'd do'. I think of how to make it change and go there… I look to the water and watch the rippled tidings sing, where the Sun has met them distant toward the sultry shore, and the little peach and pink houses on the shallow beach where the insignificance of the swallows persist flightily against the clear grains and gravelly tanned sand. I watch the light*

11

meet wind swept stability all catching to meet the light as a fish might meet their insect at the ponds top, all meeting, but its "just light", or "just waves" and each is dead until I realize that as I tell myself again that it is not "just waves". Maybe it would be "just waves", if I could understand what just one of these ripples were, but I cannot,, not even a drop, for it is life, and beyond me, and my conscious analytic experiential logic of labeling and containing...

At this moment there stood before me the little quivering shining prisms of all those things in that water that I did not know, and the more I thought about it, the less and less I knew; and the less I knew the more the lights on that pond twittered, the more they became real, the more my soul seemed almost to be able to touch them. I was there, lost in myself, and all that has that timeless ancient beauty, being part of this same miracle as I, this these Gods things, as I washed too upon this shore to fathom for a farthing the larger soul, like a Sea that we are all a part of, that conjoins us, and makes us whole by our necessary mutual fallibility.

It might be a greater ethic to be there by the water, with that Sun than even the evolutionary goal of procreation. I wish once before my death to call a monastery of eastern philosophy my home, where the meaning of this life in its simplicity may fill lungs, heart and soul, as that I may be comforted, alone in the womb, and reading the annals and mystery of history, peoples, Gods, and this matrix of absurd intrigue;
    while sitting.

Cooling Water

I viewed low from a dimpled meniscus squat that a woman and her young daughter tenderly fished along the shoreline of the beach. The brim of the mother's hat was drawn over her forlorned face and this made them look as if they were in a landscape painted by Cezanne. They waded together in the shallow protective bell curve that wrapped around the rocks and sand. It comforted me to see them so distant, knowing that they could not interrupt the coming inner voyeurism of my own world.

My kayak hovered with stillness *adrift* on the *windless* waters. I could see with clarity the lines *demarcating* the water under these steadily greying skies. There was an infinite nothingness between me and *them*. No wind carried nor *repelled* sound… just the nothing *between* us. I lit the joint, hit it and went back into the reality of the moment. I could feel the clarity of the lines pressed *smooth*, as a bed sheet made un-*rippled* against its mattress, smoothed out as the tussles in my memory, and forced into a sharper focus the steepled chimes of a youth past, misunderstood and haunting.

> *What would it feel like to be so truly alone*
> *that one had not even oneself?*
> *Whose arms indeed would touch,*
> *whose tongue and nose taste,*
> *whose eyes to show light to?*
>
> *The deepest depression mocks itself,*
> *because there is no one to listen,*
> *nor one who cries*
> *or one who hopes to be consoled*
> *or even heard;*

just the inner pain
which recedes
into what used to be a soul;
just the hurt alone.

     I can still see Brandon on our last days of school, before our Junior year came to an end; walking into History class with this look; unshaven, dark blue t-shirt (with an orange lettered inscription that read: "Shaka of the Zulus"), clean but un-tucked, long and unflattering, hair nice yet uncared for, and these thin round shades so he didn't have to look at anybody. Brandon always used to have this wide-like smile, like 'he was in on it', and he always would look at me wide eyed and wink like I was 'hip because I knew about it too'; but he didn't that day. He gazed at me, but it wasn't him,

he wasn't there any longer.

     The multi-panoply of memory revisited, like orthodontic lenses flip, and I remember how Brandon would come to Narragansett with me and my Father. He was acutely adept socially to one as distinctly not as myself. Before we'd go out for our much deserved teen-aged rabble rousing, he mentored me to his ways in dress, picking out for me what in his mind would show me in the best light reproductively-speaking; how to tuck, where, collars up, down, belts and positions of hats. All the things young men do to accentuate their phallic-nature, much as a teenage girl wears pink to accentuate her own unique sexual virtue. Then there was his sophisticated haberdashery of cologne selection, I do believe *Cool Water* was his favorite.

To a social moron such as me, any help at relieving awkwardness and discrete unease was appreciated. I always felt foolish taking the advice of my mother or sisters for whatever reason, but Brandon was like a brother I always wished that I had had. He had this uncanny confidence that would allow him to be able to spontaneously get silly, flirtatious, and be able to talk to nearly any girl anytime he wanted. I was his sidekick who was along for the ride. Brandon was the show, and he had to be. It was like somebody had injected him with an extra dose of life serum when he popped out. By the time the doctor set him to nap he was already dancing, but with this comfortable masculine-baby-like jig that not many could touch, and its not that he tried, it was just natural.

"a joke is an epigram on the death of a feeling"   *- Nietzsche*

The thoughts of Brandon *left* me, and I was *alone* again with my parents at home. How the grey had streaked down atop the crest of the *great* bird, I wondered how the seasons apart had *changed* my Father. I can see him far away sweeping the trove of dead Lady Bugs that have fallen, stilted from the batted insulation stuffed into the basement ceiling joists, where their eggs were kept warm over the last winter, then deposited into the waste barrel. Sound in his silence, alone; that part I believe I *admire* most. We used to listen to Sinatra together, alone in the car. Sometimes he *sang* the melody low like, and I wondered why he sang the words after Sinatra, and not *in-line* with him. Sinatra's voice forever *ceased* one week ago.

I can see through the bare outstretched branches, shorn of their leaves that look naked indeed, the family tree, an oak wide, full and rounding like a Ferris wheel propped and conspicuously saved from the chainsaw. I can see Mom far away, characteristically tender and anxious, seasonally gathering as if life depended on her building the nest. Maybe it is the *words-themselves* which have created the distance between us.

The street trickster plays with us a shell game; it is only the closer to *death* as we become with age, that that which has been beneath the shells is at last revealed to us. The old may look back at what became of their life awestruck at the way the events played out, and the revealing of one's own destiny. E*xistential truth is most humbling.*

How will death come; in an instant or a prolonged suffered waiting? Will we understand our last breath to be our last, or will we be caught unprepared and let it slip away unconscious of its leaving much as we fall asleep? How exactly will death be revealed unto us? Will there be *meaning* implicit within, and if it means anything at all; then will this *meaning*-something depend on others who will derive meaning from it after we are dead, or that meaning which is with us, that we live and die with? What *is it* to die for something?… to perish for something *other than life?*

Le Mountaine Sacre

It was the summer before our senior year in High School and at the end of the long hot month of June; Brandon threw a get together at one of the fella's houses. When I got there, he had the large white 'Epiphyte' cooler planted on the porch, filled with Cythonioi, (a Greek beer) and he was handing them out with this real humble, down to earth look in his eyes, the kind that would look straight past-into your own, *naked* and with no malice.

He had his *Angels* hat on backwards, but was otherwise clean looking, wearing a forest green-T with an *epigraph* of John Lennon, hanging *un*-tucked over his doughboy frame, without even the typical odd mélange of pimples that his complexion was *oft* to tender. It had made me think about going to church with him just a few weeks prior;

> his iron pressed tan slacks,
> white shirt and tie,
> contrasting with my comparatively paltry accounting
> of acceptable dress code,

sitting beside him in the pew I looked him over and he gave me this sidelong smile as he lifted his pant-sleeve to show me he had one more surprise; his wool socks which seemed almost outfits in and of themselves; he said,

> *"gotta look good for God"*.

I look back and I didn't know it then, but he was greeting me with the cold wet beer that he handed me and with his eyes that can still penetrate *my living memory*, with a sincerity, *bleeding* 'my

friend'; they were saying to me for the very last time. And with that,
"we're even now",

                        dropped clear from of his mouth.

      At some point he must have borrowed 5 or 10 dollars from me. I smiled at his gesture and his eyes, and said back, *"ok"*. He made a point of sweepingly telling the others the same, one by one as they arrived he left nobody *out*, and neither did a one think *twice* about it. That night I could see the neighbors house in his big *green eyes that shone up, to shine down an enthrallingly deep whirl-pool draining...*

                    ... oh deep many layered time.

      I had always resented his girlfriend,

                            always having to be around and taking him hen-pecked her way picking him up at my house when she wanted to, and generally making sure she's got the key to his pants. He was too much fun to be tied down, couldn't she see that? Well, they were all broken up and I was glad thinking it was going to be a real long hot summer about girls and beaches and fuckin' off.

The night hung in the air like a
holy wafer dangled, crisp
with my tongue waiting,
'Amen' and mocking *still,*
within the clutches of the high priest robed,
and robbing. 'Electra', we called her,

(the unnamed fellow's sister) came home,
as with her some *choice* handmaidens.
Everything went swimmingly for a bit,
but one of the girls had to go worship *the pot*,
and the fellow had us leave.

       I remember Brandon emptying out the large cup that the evil-conglomerate-*Taco*-place gave us, and filling it with what beers we had left. We were passing it back and forth until *a cruiser* pulled up behind us, and I'm not sure if Brandon even had a chance to think before he tossed the cup out the *window* and blessed the sidewalk with it. That was when the 'police occifer' put his blues on and signaled us to pull over. Brandon just got out of the car and started walking and the occifer, Paul who knew Brandon called after him but he *didn't stop* until he was wrestled down, *maced* and handcuffed.

       We talked on the phone and laughed about this newly acquired police record of *his*, two days after that night's events. He had always seemed to be the one able to get away, I told him jokingly, *"you're part of the gang now"*, I thought I even recognized the elation of being mildly proud of finally being the 'bad' boy.
       Something in me *sunk* down while I was listening to him, when we talked about a thing that we had been a *little mad* at each other for months-back. I felt that it had all receded into the past. His voice assured me that *"it's cool"*. He told me he'd be down for dinner with *"the fam and some b-ball"* the following night. He couldn't *"tonight cuz I'm hanging out with my moms"*, he told me as he laugh-gasped at the humor of his words.

That night when he kissed her goodnight and walked down those cellar stairs,

each *step*
the last those feet
would carry him, gracing
each of the pine treads as individually
 significant, in their Hume-ian solidity; he must
 have embraced *each* very moment that carried him, *resolute*,
 to his purpose. I can only imagine that his heart was *full* and
innocently *startled* that this great moment had finally arrived; that it
was *his* own sculpture; a sepulcher which stood before him and his
own choice; or perhaps the choice of the feeling of perpetual
mourning and sensitivity penetrating his
$$\textit{infinite-gravity-towards-implosion…}$$

No matter whose choice it was, it was Brandon who *wept* and
was to persevere unto the great undertaking of understanding and
would give up the *ghost*; it was he who transcended himself and his
experience to make *meaning* within the sacrifice, meaning with the
life before him, its moments of infinite-finiteness and with planned
calculation at once became
$$\textit{… pure and unforsaken.}$$

And how the bared chains must have dangled the *chimes* of
the mar-rying bells ringing in their *distilled subtraction*, leaving *empty*
the s-hook and the *swinging* pendulum *aperture* which held them the
object of the *pain* transferred. From around his waist he *took* off his
favorite belt from his favorite *pants*, and placed it around his neck,
'*Introibo ad altare Dei*', holding up the other end and fastening it to
the shining metal swivel, which had held his punching bag.

What beautiful eyes he had … he was finally clean of everything, and all the ones that had *abandoned him*. He would be abandoned no more, finally it would be he who would jump ship first. He showered and *cleaned* his room, taking care to throw away his collection of short stories that he read to me, "*The fascinating and slightly pornographic comic-adventures of various cripples*" and fated dark poetry; his baseball cards, music, computer and magazines all gone; floor vacuumed, shelves dusted, with but two things out of place; *he left the watch in the middle of his carpet Easy Rider style,* and his class ring he left atop his desk turned down…

I think he must have thought about the ½ dozen people closest to him and how we would just puzzle over these last moments of his and how everyone would eventually move on without him. I guess he thought it had to be. *He was clean*, and when the muscles in his legs kicked that chair out from beneath him, they were *as loose and calm as his conscience*.

His Mother said she had heard something downstairs, like a large thudding noise that disturbed her quiet reading. She called out to him "*Brandon, Brandon*". She waited too long,
                          he didn't respond, though he heard her,

        he could not. His neck was snapped.

She traced his steps down to the basement, where when arriving, she watched as his body lay *dangling* from the bared upper wooden joists in the ceiling. She took a hold of his *body*, and tried to *raise* him, so that he could *breathe* and though he had no holes in his *hands*, the weight of his body was too much towards *gravity*. Her scream whose panic and terror ripped into the *hearts* of those whose house's were near, stretched across the empty hopeless impotent *plain*, and plead for some *God* to save what she knew as her *son*... to save the *values* that he *surrendered*; because to him *he was saved*, his salvation was *his dowry and gift*.

Why would he do it with her *upstairs* in that house?

Could he have thought it would have been a more *intimate* good-bye? He probably calculated it so that she would have found him in the morning, mourning

                     ... *mourning morning*. How different is the calculation from reality? In the morning her being, conscious and unconscious might have inwardly *intuited* that he flew *fated* away in the night *painlessly* by his own choice; but finding him instead *warm and hearing* the weight of his body *break* his neck... would begin for this woman an experience of a dark

                         sleepless night of which she would never to awake from. I can only *imagine* that his Irish freckled face said, "I *loved* you mom", but he just wasn't there any longer. He preserved his body for her to keep, as his Father had done before him; a present warm wrapped with a *tied-taut-bow*. His heart said *nothing*. His soul said, "you can not hurt me any more because I give up. You simply can not *touch me* because I will not ***allow it***".

He was so strong this boy from Marion Indiana, I remember fighting with him so badly one time; he said I fouled him, and I said he traveled first so it didn't matter, (he took a train). We yelled out the teenage *logic* of our arguments like two crazed referees relentlessly battling, the one-on-one ceased, and we just battled until I said "*fuck it*", and just walked home. He was calling after me for a while; it's kind of comical now with all the time

...*past*. After all that and now he wants to play? I just shuck my head and *kept* walking up that *Mountain* of a hill of his.

Then there was the time at my house when it got so heated everyone just backed off and gave us *space*. His wild green eyes were large, and saliva *formed* foaming bubbles between the ferocious and recondite rage brewed metal tied in his teeth and the corners of his mouth. He got his face so close to my own that I could have licked it; so I asked him if he wanted to *kiss*. He shoved me, and I went back at him and shoved him, maybe he would have smiled but instead he picked up that *ball* and chucked it at me but I caught it and gave it back, and we watched each other like wrestlers testing their strength at close range aiming the orb with all the velocity our *limbs* could carry it at each others head. And neither one of us backed down because neither one of us *knew* how to, or could, and the others just watched the detonation *click*. I picked up the heavy oak chair that used to sit at the head of our family kitchen table, raised it over my head, and flung it at him with all my might, and damn near got *him*. I saw him crack a smile a little as his *eyes* got big when he saw it coming at him, he turned tail out of its path and said, *"You're crazy"*. That was the only way you could gain his respect; you had to really shock him and make him think that you were even crazier than he was, (which was at times no small task to speak of).

He *hung* there in that cellar lifeless;
> like a puppet ,
> only a piñata,
> or an effigious bag-of-stuffing;
> his body the noble Jedi robe de-clothed.

Black robed rebel
Obscure disconsolate behemoth
Suspended spiritual samurai
The Fruit of Knowledge ripened
And unhinged on the Tree of Life

Darth Vader master-apprentice double-agent
Having achieved the 11th Sephiroth
The Qabalistic abyss called Da'ath
A glyph of an eye which is said to represent Knowledge
stood with the jowls of the universe spread under him
as he looked down onto a world of Shells

Illuminating and illuminated he fell
As a spurned angel or a wary goat-demon
Azazel or Shaitan of the tribe of Yezidis
Not a true Sephiroth at all, but the absence of one,
Created artificially as an exiled Father merely "visiting".

Aleister Crowley wrote that "*the Abyss is empty of being; it is filled with all possible forms, each equally inane, each therefore evil in the only true sense of the word, that is meaningless but malignant, in so far as it craves to become real*".

But where did the word Darth Vader itself emanate from? Possibly a double entendre; one a synthesis of 'dark' and 'death' interposed,

(Here see: d a r k
                d e a t h
                d a r t h)

24

as well the hidden meaning, within the hidden Sephiroth: Da'ath;
the name Vader is derivative of the many Indo European roots, all
meaning 'Father', and as Lucas knew well the etymology of his own
name in Latin, "lux" meant light, and so the Son, is Luke, as the Sun
is Light, and mans timelessly-suspended God that walks or rides or
rolls the Sun.

      Brandon learned well Darth Vader's wisdom imparted to his
Son the "Skywalker", Not " *I am your Father*", but hidden within the
abscess:
               " *I am you farther*";

      intoned and echoing an inviolate rapture; unfolded four times
more; once as the Father removed, burdened and made dark and
unholy by the exile of his children; again as Shaitan's menace warning
to his God that through this Knowledge I will become more powerful
then you; once more that "God, Light I am your Father", and yet again
as a howl for the miscreant fated future, meaningless but for its
malignancy; enlightened, spiritless and evil.

Did Brandon tire of being made a marionette?
Carved wooden without the pulse of veins pumped through
Inert, without meaning, abysmal, and craving?
of someone else pulling the sordid un-reciprocating *strings?*;
the short sighted festering preoccupations
 of the public and how the great many

don't want to *listen* or *think* or do
anything about the way things are
or the way they are going:
the way his Mother maybe made him feel guilty

about how his Father had *left* and how it made him feel inside, like he and his future were an nuisance to her new family.

He hid himself and his melancholy selflessly behind a shit eating grin and an overbearing light heartedness. The insides that he wouldn't show were just sad, sad,

sad. I remember drinking with him on the beach; beer and Purple Passion, goofing and talking about girls and *pain* and death and *assholes*, and what we wanted to spend our lives doing. Then we found a cove within the 'Pizza Pit' and pulled the beers we had left out of our pockets for the happy ending nonchalant and "service damn it", yet surprised that we didn't pass for 21 when we were 16, laughing the whole time *drunk as fuck*. And he'd just look at you Irish-like, head *sunk* in shoulders imbibed and delirious, like 'it was a time to remember'. And we *went* to go get high with Marina in the gallery and someone said "I've lost my head", and we tried looking for this fellow's head in the cupboards and the bathroom, in the corners, and even behind all the paintings, until we caught up with our own and just *laughed*.

Brandon and I were so close, maybe one of the nights we were out our souls unbeknownst to us, agreed to trade bodies. I say this because over time, we seemed to have *morphed* into who each other was. He inwardly yearned for what he knew not; he hadn't had it so long he forgot; a *Father* and the deeper sense one gets of themselves by *having one around*; why life was like an *ocean* and why he felt the pain he did. I just wished I could have stolen some of his carefree spontaneity, the prison of his that always seemed to be so *free*. I guess we both got our wish. My sad friend

… how I loved that sad-sad friend.

I'm not really sure who I was after he took his life. I felt like

26

someone had taken everything that I had inside *me*, and just left the skin, just the shell of the beetle. It's different when someone does it to them self. If he had died in a car crash, it would have been different. We all could have just *drank* him off, and immortalized him in our young boy way. But it didn't feel like that at all. We were with him, but we let him down, and he fell, and we didn't pick him up; and he died there, in that lonely gutter,

without hope... and alone.

Life went on and all of his friends just kind of huddled together for the next couple weeks, like puppies nursing from their mother, new from the womb. A few weeks after it happened, Jeremy asked me to come up to North Adams in the Berkshires to spend the weekend with him and his girlfriend. I had never been to that part of the state and I didn't even know his girlfriend very well. I said "sure"; I needed a change of scenery and to get away from the people who knew me, and what was going on inside me. That day we left, the Sun looked *new* against the sky, like it was an old friend in spirit, *Constance*. The possibilities floated, defying *gravity* before me. Brandon was not coming back, but my own life seemed to be ever more before me; I determined that

my meaning would be my own.

There was an old timer there with a beard and *red* suspenders on, standing between the gas pumps in the *burned-out* center of town. He blended with that Sun *in-its* direction, becoming indistinguishable from it as I could not even see *his-face*. He thought Jessica was my-girl, and she might as well have been that-weekend. While the gas pumped into our tank, he played *to-us* like we were young lovers, *love-fading* and *bleeding-new*. There was something about that *old-timer*, and that harmonica,
esoteric like-the-chanting of

Gregorian monks, inexplicable…

I think they call it 'foreshadowing'. We drove off as the man watched us wave, un-phased and fading down *at-One* with the Sun… his notes lingered with-us *rolling* on that winding old-living Mohawk trail on-route 2.

Jeremy had been working as a waiter, and pulled in 400 dollars a week. That was "some cake", we assured each other on the phone. He stayed at his brother's place; a cape cod shingled condo that blended with those mountain terraced summer streets. We pulled into North Adams chasing the steep decline down and round from the fog covered peak of Mt. Greylock, reading the signs:

"slow down; hairpin turn in ½ mile";
"hairpin turn in ¼ mile";
"15mph turn ahead"; and finally
"5mph turn ahead, caution".

Then, there below us, below the settling fog
                    at the 180 degree turn in the route we could
see the entire valley as if on a peak.

We saw the surreal old soul of the old mill village; its foreign-ness was *titillating* and novel. The purple-pink-tones of the sky melted with the bleeding heart pink tone of the receding Sun; as it went down to meet the lush blue-blue-dark-green tones in the living Night Mountains. There was something in those mountains that I needed at that moment in my life as I had never needed it before. My lungs opened and filled themselves with this un-explainable new-ness life was *revealing* unto me.

That night, I slept with ethereal intent, to the opaque mellow-moon-light-rift, reflecting off the white sheets and the lighted window opening, showing the humble mountain hardwood floors, and Bob Marley clear singularly strumming the *sacred scarabs* in my soul *free* from their womb; and Jeremy and Jess in the next room rustling their sheets and bodies *softly* to the Mountain love, bubbling re-*creation* in their own springs *springing*; and me *alone*, thinking how life is *finite*, yet completely ahead of myself and entirely within my own hands. The Sun rolled up over my make shift bedding and I was comforted by that summer

nothing...

and how the shine came through those blind-ful *bluish* tinted windows so warm. I felt emancipated from all the "*that-ness*" that we seemed to shed like snakes skin behind us, *meaning itself was made free*. My chest heaved the air with a certainty of the moment:

> cloth, warm,
> irresolute and unconfirmed;
> *only confident of the metamorphosis.*

Jeremy left to-wait, and with time to burn, me and Jess left to-wade ourselves into the green wilderness high atop to find the hermitage before the '*social contract*' in the largest Mountain in Massachusetts. Jess was just a little delicate thing whose *freckles* were as big as her smile, and I could tell as her rasp got wheezier she was having a tough time with the rapid incline, so I put her compact frame on top of my shoulders and let her ride me right up the Mountain. I thought that she should have felt heavy, but I didn't even notice as I rode up that path like a Giant Elephant in India bearing its princess in a tower, just glad to have the *company* and a *tusk* to get me things. She laughed the whole time, and she made me happy to hear her laughing in that simple hearty underwater-creaky-country-way. I don't know how she and that Mountain made me forget so-*completely* the rest of the outside world, its reality and past… but they did.

We wandered amidst the high grasses and paths, looking out at stretches and turning back to see the city *obscured* by the patterns and the farms chop-blocked casting aside the *significance* of the housing and the people in the villages, by the more overarching theme of the *insignificant vastness of everything*. And we wondered how like a dream it was to be there, and how like a dream it was we had to leave, but like the cocoon of the womb, we thought our gestation period a content one to rest, what with Jeremy out until after "closing". I walked about and saw the strokes, and as the wind blew *forth*, nature~trem~~bled, and I saw the nature moving *alive* with as many colors as a palate could *hold*, and each squeezed true from its tube, clumped oil smears hued and each path down- another Van Gogh-hewn mound, and the Sun was in everything and breathed life in all. We meandered through God's *wild*-flowered, fauna, moss, and herb, partaking of our own special blend to keep *it-all-in-perspective*. The moon-lit veil began to descend the dressing down; the show was nearing *completion*.

Our procrastination caught up to us and we decided *to awake*. Our boots trekked confident that the paths they followed would lead us down *the Mountain* but they only led us back around to themselves. This went on for *hours* until we couldn't see any further than the foggy 4 feet before us and barely that. The coyotes were *howling* frightening discontent adding to the uncertainty of the circumstances. By the time it was midnight, (*and we rolled Easy Rider style*), we had been in the mountains for 13 hours.

It was so hot that Jessica had taken off her shirt to aerate her bosoms, leaving only her off white bra on. I had taken off my shirt as well, to feel the brisk-*cool*-Mountain wooded air that she spoke of. Between the heat and the *mosquitoes*, the dark, and the coyotes, we knew we had problems. Down the mountain we looked round and round and we searched for anything on the ground that we could pin point and use as our *compass*. Then we saw it, a light some distance away, yet a light and so therefore life and electricity. The light itself became our beacon and we followed its lead as if a path

floating

abstract over all the *vicissitudes* that a ground path would eliminate effortlessly. We saw nothing but we knew that the moon was to our back because directly in front of us was darker then to *either* side.

We swung down as jungle folk might have, in younger evolutionary moments, clinging together the *forbidden* lust within our bare and sweaty bodies, holding onto each other as we slid down areas too dangerous to walk or swing. We followed that light for 3 hours straight down the mountain and when we hit bottom, we didn't care about anything. Jessica and I looked at each other like we never had before and nor ever again. We shared *that Mountain* that night and the closeness and struggle to make it back.

Walking along the road we could feel the inter-spirit vibrations of our lives more *clearly* connected to our mortality and choice. The strength of our spring though exhausted was reborn with a fertility and certainty of a purpose unknown. A giant black horse must have smelled us and followed us along the line of the road, for as far as his fence allowed him. What surprise for him to see the figures unmasked from the Mountain base emerge, filtered as *walking shadows* exposed.

At last we came to a house and farm that shone the light from the outstretches of a solitary horse barn. We rattled at the door till we heard a fellow come down surprised to see as he did, two filthy kids at 4 in the morning. We told him our story and asked to use his phone. To this day I have never tasted more delicious, more cooling water in my life than that which was brought out by that man, and as I looked into those two large fattened glasses,
  I vanished into my thirst
     squelched.

Lotus Blue

An old blue kite string
and ribbon saunters guiding
the clear water running

as it presses gently over
rocks smooth to the wear,
feeding into the nurturing

mellow wet valley of the lotus.
The lotus is made warm
by the yellow Sun on high;

Beadle Scat

laid cool by the darkened
muddy mottled waters
on low. The two spin fast

like a children's fan
breath blown;
it is that child

who may see through...
The petals of the lotus
are the smooth, soft,

fruit dressed for the dance.
The colors of the trees
freed fallen float

amongst the season's
last chance prance.
Left in the sift,

a deft silt drift;
it leaves and cleaves
to the mottled

muddy leaves so
that some day
when the time

conceives, they
may again give life
to the lotus.

Southern Massachusetts

The breeze blows cool through soaked leaves high, dripping, air born-flighted mini-drops as their branches sway, with the dark wet rainy wind. For the last 3 years I have not spent more then a month at a time here at home in Massachusetts. It feels familiar though different; I think because I am different. I felt *the nothing* again… two days ago in my Father's office. I saw my sister Renee and smiled. She smiled back. Sometimes I think that she lives in it
                                        … *there.*

It's not something that really can be said. It feels light, *like clouds* when you're

                                        … *there.*

On my way home, I walked into a local donut shop to grab a coffee for the ride home. I longed to see a person, so I went in. The *uniformed girl's plain face smiled as I was leaving* and said, "Have a good day". I said back "you too", and walked out. Even the seconds seemed to be worlds in themselves if I didn't try to control them, if I could be humble enough to just let them be. Why would I even want to have a 'good' day, if I could have a day in which I could experience the simple eternity that lies *within our finite moments*?

Just to be riding along these *roads* again, the way the
headlights led softly into the gently curving old-country-roads, past
quit'n time in old factories and the quiet small town suburbia,
illuminated what would be for me a meaning

... that was a becoming.

The wipers against my windshield started to cry-shrieking
that the rain had cleared. My chariot appeared to have stopped within
the lighted clearing of a parking lot belonging to an ice cream depot
not far from my house. From the outside window I could see the
young girl moving fastidiously rolling her giant balls onto the waffled
cones so that they sit side by side. Her brown hair was bunched up and
attractively held within an amulet-clasp bearing what looked to be a
ceramic beetle with wings outstretched, *turquoise* in color.

She had on a black shirt and tan shorts, and as she leaned
over to scoop my ice cream, my eyes took hold of her rump, so
sensuously formed. I could see that when she turned around that her
eyes glistened with the youthful lust that knew too well where my
own eyes had just been. She handed me my dark jimmy crowned
coffee laden waffle, so I smiled but her smile back made me timid and
weary for a comfort which had eluded me in times past. My ice cream
came to $3.46 so I let her keep the change, and I went and sat on the
bench in front and ate it, alone, and let the thoughts and sounds of the
street and people waiting in line ***Passover***
Me

Clean

Empty cogitation chasing
bird shit on sill sitting
before me as I in
my solemn wooden chair ache.

What if life had been different?
the burly drops of rain
show their wares
wearing heavy on my sill shit.

*Grey skies donning
make the morning mist
reveric in its solitary confinement
And so I am led around*

*as my mind chases,
chasing my mind chasing...
this life:
what more could I have done?*

*Still-ly the motionless St Anthony statuesque
that sits in the corner presents itself
between the bureau and my bookcase.
I remember taking up reading*

*when the worldliness and reality
s h a t t e r e d
and I experienced my-self
to be no more.*

And when I came back from college the first thing I did when I got home was to take down the mirror from atop the dresser bureau, for it *repulsed* me. I remember a time when I was so proud of that mirror. When I got to High School, I taped the pictures of all the people I thought were my friends to it until I was barely able to see my own face in it.

> I don't know why I had to take it down.
> Maybe I didn't like *the-me* in the pictures,
> maybe I didn't understand my smile,
> perhaps I was disappointed in all those people
> ~I thought were my friends.
>
> Maybe I was just sorry it all had to end,
> but it did,
> and it didn't really matter why.
> I didn't want to look into that reflection
>   ~and those photos and be seduced
>   ~to believe that the images that I saw were me.

> *I knew I had changed*
> *and it seemed simpler*
> *with so little there.*
> *The simplicity itself*
> *seemed clean.*

I didn't have to look at all those people I had grown up with, doing all the things that didn't matter to me anymore. They were living different lives now and I had to go on with my own. For the first time, I had a TV in my room. I placed it on this bureau and next to it an Italian statue of Christ,

and a *framed*
 picture of
my *Father*, tanned,
with these *shades* that made

him *look*-like
he belonged in one of the Godfather *flicks*,
*(*leaning against a protective railing*)*,
over-looking the Bar Harbor waters in Maine.

Next to my Father's picture I placed my three favorite stuffed animals growing up. They were presents that my Father brought back from the Islands. When I was a kid, I found that I could play Monopoly with them. I really liked Monopoly growing up; I think because I liked the colored money, and the way my imagination could make it worth something, even for a little while in the other world within my mind. Its funny though, all the times I played with my stuffed animals I can't remember nearly as well as the two times that my Father played with me. I can still remember 2 ones were 'snake eyes', 2 twos 'busy bees', *and **if you got 2 fives you had "rolled the Son"**.*

Thinking

My thoughts seemed to run like an errant ball disfigured, and I wobbly after it. Even if I tried to not-think, I couldn't. I stut*ter*ed when I talked, Mom says because I couldn't spit the words I wanted to say out fast enough. I remember lying on my back in my bed for hours upon end before ever being able to sleep. While awake, I watched how the light would play with the shadows upon the dimpled white painted plaster ceiling, all the time *thinking*.

When Dad and Mom would send me to bed, I'd say: "why, I won't get to sleep for another three or four hours anyway?" However after a while I took to liking bed time because its reality was not shaped by any one other than me; I was its sole adventurer, it belonged *to me alone*. My imagination was not constricted by adult standards in neither thought nor deed.

At times,
I would take to wondering
about how life would be,
about how it was that I was alive at that time,
and how *time* would never again be the same,
nor I. The *passage*

of time existed all around me, as an envelope does its letter. I wondered how strange it would be to feel as one felt when dying. How accurate could I be, a simple boy of 5 knowing nothing of the complexity of how time affects man? But I was curious, and I thought my imagination could carry me there. How would I feel on those fated days, with only hours looming before me?

> What if I could transcend time so as to smile
> and wink at my elder dying me at the moment,
> would it not all seem as though in a dream?
> *Could I feel this life and death within me,*
>
> *profoundly so as to project me now; later as a laugh?*
> How great would be the laugh if I could glance
> within myself dying, and see the young me
> *looking back at me having known me*
> *and this moment all along?*

When I went to bed, I entered a place of holiness. It made me giddy not ever knowing where my mind would take me, and how it seemed somehow magical- like something was working by itself; *thought chased after thought.* My ideas would give way to other ideas, and theories, and questions and more questions until I realized how much I didn't know, but also how far along my own mind could lead me. My world circled with ideas, I still remember *loving* ~ simply being able to *think.*

One night I had the thought, "how did I ever begin thinking about this?" I wondered and arduously,

> as coupled fetters bound
> I traced back
> my chased track,
> as if sun-dirt *one by one*;

.

At times I would go back a dozen links or more to find out what I was originally thinking of. If I accomplished this, and reached the first idea from which all other ideas emanated, I experienced a pleasurable feeling of having been freed, maybe by having seen the topographical outlook of the cognitive labyrinth.

My dream world began as relatively simple, much as any other boy of my age. When I awoke I was surprised by the happenings within my dream world, but took them rather in-stride. It wasn't until a dream became re-occurring that I thought much about the whole process. I guess I found that it was rather strange that my mind could be forgetful enough to be fooled by the same dream *twice*.

The dream was of a scientist who scoured the house with his dog, apperently intending to do some harm to myself. I in turn, would hide in the den behind the beat-brown easy-boy, on the dirty-beat-brown carpet and survey as they strode repeatedly past the den's outer threshold. I pulled back a secret latch, and escaped through a passageway behind the sofa that led to a ladder receding down into the cellar.

At some point, after the third or fourth time I had this dream *I reflected; "how absurd is this dream of mine?"* I should have recognized that I was dreaming but the thought never came to my mind, even after having the same dream again and again. It made me feel foolish and I wondered if I could train myself to recognize when something was absurd, to ask if I were dreaming. I began by asking myself whilst awake the question

"Is it real? Is it real? Is it real?",
over and over again while accomplishing menial tasks.

What intrigued me possibly the most about dreaming was the experiential *"thrown-ness"* to use Heidegger's phrase; the fact that everything in a dream appears as though it were reality. What was this reality? Was I not looking at the actual *innards* of my own unconscious mind? (What-ever-is-me); could I be conscious of my unconsciousness, able to watch it as a curiosity rather than being at its will?

Often what we take for granted in our dreams are the transition points. All of a sudden we are thrown into a different reality, and we **react** to it, rather then **question** the actual transition point: *"how the hell did I get here?"* If you are not able to trace your experience back through a series of logical memories, chances are you are creating the very environment you are reacting to. If this is so, and you created the scene and the players, you could also change the scene, the players, and the plot.

Eventually, enough time passed and with it enough training for the battle with my own mind; when the moment arose I was ready. My unconsciousness had thrown me into a reddish tinted negative room. There I met the horror films' own Freddy Krueger and as you may know it is within the dream itself that Krueger comes to kill his victims, the dream of which there is no escape. I thought: *'this is weird. Where in God's name did he come from?'* Then I figured it out;

I was dreaming.
    I looked around to
        realize what I saw
            was an illusion
                created within
                    my own mind.

I looked around, and back at him as if he was merely a part of a game that my own mind had created to amuse or terrorize itself. As I looked around to see things as they actually were, this apprehension of the illusion gave me complete control of the situation. He could do nothing to hurt me because irregardless of what happened, I was shortly going to wake up in my bed. But this did not satisfy me. I lusted to beat him, and reclaim the thrown of my own mind. This image of that fearsome Freddy we have come to know looked visibly shaken, like 'the gigs up'. It was my very fear that he thrived on, when withheld, he appeared anemic, feeble and weak. I thought "if only I had a weapon", so I looked around and somehow my unconsciousness must have created an electric outlet that Krueger was plugged into. I simply pulled the plug and out he went.

There is nothing quite like being aware enough in your dreams to fly anywhere you please. Beyond lucidity, it offers the style of non-conflict where if your mind manages to have an enemy about, you can just fly away and it doesn't matter. What colors would emerge; what people and the sensation of flying through crowds, so untouchably. Still quite young, I remember waking up, and trying to remember the thoughts that carried themselves by succession 8 or 10 hours before, and count them back as if it were the night. I found that with some determination, I could in fact do this, *almost.*

The problem was that I never could remember the last thought I had before I was asleep. Once I had a point I could go either way, *forwards or backwards,* but I never could remember the single thought directly before I went to sleep and I couldn't understand why. So it *eluded* me, and thus it challenged me. I became more conscious of my interior dialogue. What I mean when I say this is that I thought about the things my mind chased after, but still I watched my own mind chase, curious as to the very process of thinking itself.

The nights that followed did not in themselves solve this dilemma. It was in fact years later when some more seasons had helped calm and mature my quest. Then, when I was ready, it came to me: going to sleep is not something someone actually thinks, nor are they able to think it because it *is actually happening* to them, and before it happens physiologically to one's body, the mind itself shuts down.

This is why I could not remember my last thought, because even before the rest of my body; my mind itself was in the process of shutting down. When the realization comes that one is going to sleep, it is a Highlander-esque 'quickening' process that takes place. If one is aware of this, they may just understand it to be a pleasurable and calming experience and that is all. It is perhaps because to understand this on the intellectual level and watch your mind going to sleep transcendentally, it is an entirely different sensation altogether. It requires a complete reversal of the physiological process in and of itself.

In order for one to be aware and conscious of going to sleep, they must first suppress this knowledge enough so that they can look inside their own sleeping body in a place like purgatory itself; not quite awake nor yet quite asleep. If one becomes aware that their mind is actually going to sleep, they will either let it as probably happens in 98 % of the cases, or the thought itself will awaken them. Several hundred times I tried to stay within this thought, actively while the rest of my body shut down only to be awakened by this unusual request. Then it happened as if an orgasm of spiritual dimensions. It was a quiet compromise of the obstinate and the subordinate; a power of the soul *sheered* through like the scene from the movie 'Flatliners' come alive; where the medical students search to find out what the after-life is like by voluntarily dying for a few minutes. The moment my soul leaped into this union it crossed a great white expanse of being, a

l i m i t l e s s n e s s
"Vvvvvooooooohhhhhmmm", the whiteness stretching seemed to sound.

My soul and mind were One in this fascinatingly interesting land, leaving behind my body to sleep by itself. How strange to have the New World's shores so close yet for the greater part of time... so in-assessable, like the moon docked to the earth's port of call, which no ramps could be placed... Could I sustain this, could I create within this? Could I live such that, I could experience even that time that my body lay recuperating? Is it possible that I could I die early having recuperated never fully in sleep? Would it be possible at all to accomplish this? to bridge the massive gape of eternity that lies within oneself?

I think that there could be what some Parapsychologists would refer to as "other plains" of existence. We see life from our own person. The psychologists say that we are somewhere between what we learn and what we are genetically encoded to be. This is how we live; the expression of the interplay and rebellience between the love of life, and the love of pain and death.

But why could there not be other plains, within the same space, perhaps covened by spaces curve; a plain of hyper space and inter-dimensionality transcending our normal waking experience; coupling the communicative capabilities unforeseen and

unknown to known life.

Time itself could literally stop within its reveling thrown Mass; a place *where the spirits ability to create is heightened so that that actually becomes the existing reality*; a place where the astral body is light, where the will is strong; with others, yet where the sensation of the empty *aloneness* itself *exudes;* a place of places, a portal to dimensions unknown, a being amassed within our own but covered by the subterfuge of our own ego, a threshold to eternity, to spirits, to beyond

and to our very soul.

Salty Dung

She came to me in the night.
Effortlessly we flew with haste.
Where?
Somewhere,

in our own space,
by the car in our hearts
and the dewy grasses
of our souls;

I was there.
I said who are you?
She was the bare freshest vision
staggering through

the light speed of space
that can be only love.
She asked me the same
but I did not know my name,

I could not think of it,
(perhaps I didn't or don't have one),
However, hers was
Anastasia.

I told her that I could not stay.
"Why?" she rejoined.
I could not answer;
I kissed her only,

holding close her body
to me and thinking
 of the limitless possibilities
there.

Surely, this is life.
The other is death.
I left to realize
myself in bed.

"I contradict myself? Very well then, I contradict myself."
~ Mohatma Gandhi.

    Of all the sins of industrialization, maybe the greatest is the archetypal myth of man to be cohesive, constant and coherent in character; as that of one who must realize a self (stable and inert enough to claim yet it is the same self) throughout his experiences, and his thoughts and feelings regarding them. This serial monotony of self-ful-ness deadens something within us. Every time another looks at us, they look *further* in knowledge instead of the *humility more close to our being.* Every time we realize *us* through this myth of self, and others that have amalgamated themselves into this

logical-biological, man-myth, cohesive-confluency;
here- the need to be a constant,
to be ambitious; to do,
to use our selves and our lives:
much as our thumb became the tautological tool:
as one seeks to control,

one is controlled by the very desire to control;
that which manipulates and that which is manipulated
by it's own manipulation, hence not an end in itself;
here: 'sprawling on a pin';
here: 'formulated in a phrase',
with no recourse to the question,

*"what really are we,
and what is really going on?";*

If only one could scuttle sideways across the ocean floor ala
Prufrock as a *'pair of ragged claws'* we would be fortunate indeed;
our own fate is more likened to a two headed turtle, each head at one
end of the shell, each with a set of front legs, each sharing but one set
of hind legs, their entrails and a tail between them.

We move as if our actions were self propelled yet are as if
dictated by the actions of another end of us that we know not, nor
have access to except by the shit we share between us. As the
movements of the dung beetle are a product of the dung it transports,
had this turtle to hold the earth atop it, it would be best to

"sit and make progress in this",

but alas in absence of words and the tools of communication, how would one best bridge the gap and at last whose front paws will end up in the shit?

When I have risen, as *Khepri rolling*, to find myself perplexed in my own self-contradictoriness that this is life, and the other that I have left is death; I am aware of the other, and its achievement of meaning and yet I am thoroughly exhausted, through its attainment. I can not go back; 'the light is too bright', for me *now.* How can one look else-how? This is not but a training facility, for the battle of the soul elsewhere,

there where the possibilities merge with... love...
there where feeling itself says;   *this is it.*

Within these awakenings;
and in *that*, which I may not speak of
ushers forth the question, "what is worth doing?",
("doing" or "dung"?, I'm perplexed).
What thought is worth *chasing* after,
what belief or feeling worth holding,
which places to fly from, to,
and where would one conceptually even begin?

What is the meaning of meaning?
Could it be captured within a feeling?
Possibly attributable to a "*this is ness*"?
We all must chase after meaning,
through thought, and feeling.
In every act, every stir, every
insipid comment, we chase.

When we rise for work, we rise for meaning;
we chase, to regain, and hold onto this "*is*-ness".
We may forget,
for as chasing does cause us to be forgetful,

a single object, the experience of color,
perhaps a shade of carpet, tan, of innocence lost,
of timelessness lost, of our own death impending.
Life is a lover we know we must lose, *someday*.
How can we squeeze this love that will leave us,
feeling a fool? Life, death,
they are *the same, and different*.

They are us. Separation of the two ideas,
one into good, and the other into bad equals fruitlessness.
They are our destiny and the only things
that we may rightly call *our own*.

She came to me in the night, and swept me up
to fly alongside her... in *that air*. I knew I must leave,
yet I knew that there was something there,
in my feelings,
an "is-ness" that I would not go back
to in most moments. I knew it was *exceptional*.
And when I rolled over rising,
I realized it was too exceptional
for this consciousness.

Frames

The boy stood *taut* atop the newly framed first deck of the house with me. He was about the same age as me, but he had the face of a boy. His figure was bony thin; it appeared almost emaciated. I wondered why his body was not composed of more muscle. Amongst the others he seemed not to belong. His shirt was plaid with stripes of red and white. It *glistened* with the February air of New England that laughed at the snow and promised the spring would soon arrive. His eyelids squinted but he was looking in my direction. The Sun on him reflected to me, a refreshingly simple smile, one that wore well with his freckle be speckled face. Somewhere within me, I felt a need to know what it would be like to live his-life, to be inside his-body, and see as he sees things. I knew if I could, then maybe I would understand my Father better,

and thereby understand myself.

I studied how he would layout the 2 x 4's that would emerge as the back wall. Lining each stud up with its own predestined x, gazing down it, assuring himself it was straight and not bowed, or if so crowned towards the sky. Then, balancing himself with one foot holding down the wall stud, he nailed it into the sole plate, its predestined soul mate. His body and head still; concentrated, his shoulder in an instant separating itself in motion from the rest of its *composed perpendicularity of posture*, floating a long necked iron 20 ounce clawed-hammer back, then in one motion, following *through*; the wrist snapping to finish the head of the nail off. His swing is easy, like cutting a slice of cheese. I could see he even relished pounding two sewn pieces of wood, and making them conjoined into one. Each-to-each, he made his way into the valley of the wall.

I wanted to tell him about *the possibilities…* about what people have done, and what he could do, discover, or be, and how he wasn't who he thought he was, but he was distant amongst his own more secure surroundings in the world that he knew. He turned his head and looked upon my face. The Sun shone through near blindingly, his sincerity of expression and with it a half smile, he riddled me; *"but I'm a framer, that's what I am, it's all I know"*.

How there on that day, on the up-righted slatted joists we stood and I could feel the timelessness of the craft and there breathed the crisp morning air over looking the other houses and homes and I wondered what following in the steps of a Jewish carpenter and foot soldier of God really meant.

The many meanings of the verb *'to frame': a system or structure of enclosure, general or specific, that gives support; and/or the creation of such a structure either physically or metaphorically, figuratively or actually, through perception, cognition, rhetoric or instinct.*

I couldn't think how to express myself, yet I knew if I had to live with such a simple answer, then that which was inside of me would be a vomitous fester pool, nauseous and acidic to the core. I retaliated, (part out of desperation, for I knew I could not convey to him what I meant), *"but you're not just a framer, you're a human being…*

who can choose". I felt as though I had lost the battle. I could not break through *to connect*.

53

I tried to think how it might be to call someplace my home. I felt as though my life were a smooth-sand

b e i n g – s i e v e d
t h r o u g h-f i n g e r s
w h i c h – w e r e
n *o* *t* - *m* *i* n *e*.

My future was uncertain; my desire for family, *for-us-traded*. I longed to rise next to a beautiful girl, who would/could nurture with me a garden true, children, grown healthy and able to love still and a cozy house on the water.

It was more or less just an archetypal throwback to the way life was supposed to be, that I still wanted to somehow believe in; regardless there seemed to be too many possibilities to decide before one compromised oneself to weekend baseball games on the tube and light beer. Life is far too blown apart to settle so easily for any one solution, not at this age. I wanted to scream to him

the possibilities
... but it was at last impossible.

I thought about the Mountains of West Virginia; white water rafting on the Deerfield, and the look on Moishe's crystal blue eyes when we hit a rock and she went over into the drink; the sense of exhilaration you get rowing in a crew craft synchronized in motion with 7 others and how when it *felt* right it was like a machine launching you through the blue depths, low-like-in ancient Viking lore; the way the ancient New River bended flowing and how everything looked small when standing on that rustic old bridge that looked out at the great gorge; the camp and people at 'Suc Lic' in

Lewisburg to whom I am forever referred to as Chainsaw Mike;
reading all the great thinkers in Stump's 'Socrates to Sartre' for the
first time, Philosophy Societies, groups and classes, and asking
tedious questions that usually only the professor, myself, and perhaps
one other in the room would or could appreciate; the *depth-silence* and
serious appreciation Professor Newomb gave the deepest and most
complex dialectical reverberations echoing from soul to ears, for
which he had no answers but would tell me to

> *"keep working on it"*;
> to the beatific soul
> of one great Jack Keruoac
> flying in his Buick from coast to coast,
> and the Gulf to anywhere USA
> with his buddy *Dean Moriarity*
> for 7 years
> and then to write *'On the Road'*
> in 3 weeks
> with pages taped together
> so he never had to stop to put the
> paper in-to the recalcitrant old type-writer.

His voice resonated through my mind like a snare drum
rapping incomprehensible rat-tap-taps:

> "I'm a framer",
> "I'm a framer",
> "I'm a framer"
> ... and I wondered,

> *who am I?*

Any attempt to elucidate on this epic conundrum; to limit, label, or otherwise capture the other side of this formulated equation met with a steep inclined, oil-slicked, oxygen-poor resistance. When we talk about what a thing *is* we are usually referring

to *its use*,   or   *what it does*.

It is through pragmatic epistemology that we understand a table is equivalent to what its purpose is. So how do we understand a thing if we know not the purpose of the thing?

How do we measure, define, comprehend,
and convey the extraordinary unique experience of
something, namely our own lives which owe to no other
purpose, but are ends-in-themselves?

After laboring in earnest perhaps my whole life trying to grasp the nature of this question, I believe *it is merely a refraction hugging for a moment off waters shown clear a reflection of a narcissistic misunderstanding; later to as a turtle might swim beneath make dark and indiscernible.* At the crux of the portal is our utilitarianistic based sentence structure. The word "who" presupposes within it an "I"; and what the "I" portrays to one is a sense of personality, (personas or ego).

'Personas' is the Greek word for 'mask', and in the Dionysian theater the mask the actor donned, was consubstantial to the thespian 'persona' he channeled. Thus, the etymological root of personality is a mask that we know each other by; a complex caricature of being and understood-ness within a social confine, minus for the greater part the essential elements of existential angst and weariness.

The problem with our personality being who we are is that it is inextricably associated, interwoven and consubstantial with how we know ourselves within the cult of our own people. The mass of men whom experience this question posed upon the universe expect to relate to others within a common understanding which they share regarding the particular rules, castes, and ritualistic expectations that become the norms for the faceless Joe's and Jane's among us (including us). The "who" within "who am I?" is incomplete in that it ignores the more fundamental question; that we are alive *prior* to our caste and the presumptiveness of any particular grouping of people by geography, nation, race, or state; and our estimation of where by the values of others, (be they alive or dead), that we fit in.

We must not allow ourselves
to have the meaning ascribed
within our own lives

to be the creation of others.
We ourselves must be the authors
of this alone.

How then could we rephrase this our necessary ontological rambled wanderings? perhaps: "what is this life?" This seems to have the advantage in having fewer presuppositions, however it serves to objectify that which is subjectively experienced, and by objectifying it; puts life in the category of a thing; which deems that it is possible to deduce its pragmatic purpose to ourselves, and not the transcendental *fly on the wall* that we experience our selves within the universe to be. It takes away the existential realness of our own feeble impotence to depend on any agency to relieve us of the angst that we feel when we alone must choose as to what the meaning of our universe will be.

So it is that the question of existence lies somewhere between a "who" and a "what", but beyond both. Maybe the most elemental ingredient is the "*how*" of our being. That is; the questions of "who" or "what" seem to defer to the primordial

> *"why are we rather than not?"*

It could so easily be the other way, yet so it is… It is the amazing enigma of causality; why exactly are we allowed to wonder who we are in the first place? If everything is the result of something else before it, how could there be anything at all?

> *It doesn't make any sense.*

Narragansett

The room that Marina and I shared sat heavy on the third floor and had a view serenaded, that stretched out across the bay golden-tan. *Crisp* white cresting waves formed-breaking and thrashed against the ancient Indian lagoon. Silently, over and over as they crashed mutinously, I viewed from high atop my bunked bed.

Down there with the leaves, where the cold air is good against the face, there is a song that tames my salty heart. It plays like the Indians did… (how in the ether) that day. It lives in me, and I take it as it sings to me … *sometimes*. Alone I sat on the swing and the peace, like the soul of a still lake, filled me. The *moan* of the night sway, like the boards of an *old ship*, slowly, *echoing* the passage *of time* beneath me.

At night when the beach was my only company, I felt *solace* in the rotating light whose shadows graced the walls of my room every 10 or so seconds. The lighthouse shone flashing round, showing itself, its mystery, our achievement, *our loneliness*, and our silence, in the pale white plastered walls from which I on the top bunk *lay perched*.

> *The space around me,*
> *my myth;*
> *absorbed the dance,*
> *the questions,*
> *the silence and the anticipation:*
> *life bleated as sheep,*
> *echoing magic*
> > *… as I became myself.*

Through my window screen, between the solitary car movements, and the distant stretches of impaled darkness came the sounds of the

> *foghorn*

and the black guy cross-legged on the sea wall, sitting *sandy*, junked out, and *alone*, with his *sounds*, mimicking the sea gulls with his echo *cry*. His sounds filled our ears, and my *imagination*, of what life is, and does to people; what people *become* and how in my days

and star wars action figures I was safe as a child, but not forever. It was weird what life did to people,

> how everyone was different,
>> and how everyone was the same;
>>> *caught in it.*

In the day there were shops lined all along the first level of every condo. It felt queer so close in proximity to so many people, like an oasis and a purgatory at one stroke. Across the street from the marketplace, two fat girls worked the Bess Eaton. Donna was the real big one with curly blonde hair and glasses. Priscilla was the *smaller* brunette one. They owned the place, and to see them, one believed it.

On the weekends, we would get a half dozen corn muffins and Dad would cook them with butter on the grill. They loved me there; they would even let me buy my sister Marina's cigarettes. After the first summer, Marina was raped at college, and she decided never to go back to her classes. She chose self-exile in this marred marring foreign land by the sea. It took on for her the duality of personality that was

> *becoming her.*

For Marina, the summer represented the necessity of having to live with other people, within the false pretense of understanding one another's lives. *The winter breeze* blew its hard freezing cruelness over the ocean plain, coldness that one could feel as even the heat in one's bone marrow became depleted. I wondered why anyone would choose to live there in the winter. It was barren, no shops, no ice cream, and so few people. It became for her a soulful reprieve *in mourning of the dialectical misunderstandings of human kind.*

It was Understanding itself that she seemed to have been *running* from. In the summer she took the company of *tourists*
passing-through
town; in the winter she took the company of *herself*. She estranged herself from her family and all the people she grew up with. The feeling of another invading one's nearest and closest sanctum of space; the treasure of evolutionary property is for the individual an extended crushing pain, which sunders from them a hope which redeems. It is for this reason an offence most grievous.

She wouldn't tell her family his name, *though she knew it well*. Caught in a feeling of guilt that knows not understanding, she killed a part of her; as she killed the baby of his that was growing inside *her womb*; she killed her hope and her own felt innocence. Her life was already over; she was just walking around

and goofing on stuff.

At the time she had taken to feeding a mutt Labrador (that we called a 'fat beagle' cause he had spots), whose owners had left in the cold for him to wander and fend for himself. His name was *Barney*. He liked Marina very much. *They filled the holes each other had*; she to him gave kindness; he to her gave an understanding that did not judge.

Everybody *seemed* to know Barney. When the weather got better, the people at the Laundromat were used to him just lying out in front of the fan, *beating the heat*. He had a whole schedule. In the morning he'd go see Donna and Priscilla for the crusted old donuts that were slated for the waste barrel and he devoured them voraciously, and so appreciatively that they looked forward to his coming back every morning.

During the summer days he would wander nearly a half mile to the *scent* of an Italian eatery, Terminisi's. They knew him like he was a regular and shoveled for him the leftovers that would have been disposed of otherwise. The night was the highlight; it was when the theater goers would come out for ice cream, and to shop in windows. Barney would wait patiently, with blood hounding hungry eyes, drooling as he watched children who might either drop their *creamy scoops*, or dip them low enough so that he could get his lap in, and after the first lap, the kids parents would just give Barney the ice cream, not knowing where his tongue had been. He probably cleaned up 2 or 3 ice creams on a slow night, possibly even 5 or 6 on a real good night. *That* was Barney.

In Narragansett, situated so closely to store units without adequate access to the beachgoers that were needed to sell their wares, me and Barney started an advertising firm; that is we went to talk to the people and asked them if they would give us money, if we put their store logo painted on a sign that we would carry and walk around in places that the beach people would see. My Father was worried someone was going to run off with me, but it never happened. Barney and I were *in-separ-able*.

He would follow me doggedly loyal all the way to the grocery store, than waiting stand on the automatic door pad so he'd get a *breeze* of the cool conditioned air that rebutted the summer heat. I heard many a customer gawk and laugh even, commenting on how smart the dog must be. Barney rolled without a leash; self controlled and self sufficient. He even looked both ways before crossing roads.

When that first summer with Barney ended, we had to say goodbye, professionally like good friends. We didn't 'own' him, even though he would have rather stayed with us. Marina kept him well cared for with the vegetable diet she offered. He went back to his old schedule, inter-sparsely spending time with her, as well as trying to beat the cruel winter that his 'owners' thought that he'd find a way to 'make it'.

When the following summer arrived, we again became inseparable, even sleeping in the same bed. Virtual replay of the entire last summer, with one change; when it ended and we were about to leave, my Mom said "fuck it, we're taking him back with us", shoved him in the car and put a blanket over him, and off we went forever to be known as the bandits that kidnapped Barney. Back in Massachusetts Barney roamed free in the acres upon acres of forest laden woods, and cryptic laid haunts and trails and rabbits and a cat that he loved so much to chase up into that wild high Oak.

Echoes of the air humming

I would dip the plate of Oreos she gave me into her short antiquitous glasses filled with cold milk. She would keep her milk in a glass jug within the fridge so that when she poured it out it was colder, and tasted better than any other milk I've ever had in my life. After that rapscallion of a mutt-poodle (Mo Mo she called him) settled down, then I would sit on her brown dog-haired-covered coach, and the front door would be left open so as to let the air come in through the seared panel screen in the creaked-out aluminum swinger, with the fan blowing and study the way my ears would get used to the evening game shows over the sound of hot air *oscillating*.

While eating those Oreos dipped in cold milk I thought how strange *time* was, looking forward while looking backward all the same, that while I was so innocent, she was 'on her way out', as my Father would say. I looked at her with great respect, and sorrow because I knew that though alive Nana and Mo Mo were on that day, that someday they both would be gone, and so I tried to appreciate the feeling and the hum of that fan blowing the moments of our lives, the dog hair and dust saturated carpet, and the love I could feel.

And that fan hummed....

Something in me wanted to emblazon those moments into the silent sanctity and the lockbox of my soul; that afternoon's fleetingness amid the dusty humid arid slow dying day that lingered on the way days used to when I was a boy without worries or things to do. I wanted to take something out of that day that nobody could ever take away; a piece of time that I could go back to and sit like I did that day, and feel just the way those cushions felt, and the way she would hide her phone underneath the magazine bookcase, how her feet would shuffle, and her slippers sounded on her way to the kitchen, or when she would try to get up she couldn't but she'd smile and say "my leg's asleep".

She didn't have many words. She didn't need them. I suppose she figured that she didn't have any use for them or that they just got in the way. Maybe she thought they didn't matter, or maybe she just

tried to make the most out of what she had; to absorb all the life
around her *till she wasn't anymore*. She had a long suffered Gandhi-
esque quality about her.

> *I wanted to hear that*
> *fan's motor hum forever;*
> *the song of us*
> *and that single day.*
>
> *I knew that I could not*
> *have even that,*
> *even my memory must yet*
> *be flawed and un-whole;*
>
> *incomplete, bare all*
> *but the passages of her is-ness*
> *and a compromising imagination*
> *that knows not where and what*
>
> *is compromised in my memory*
> *of my dear sweet Nana,*
> *her Mo Mo, and that*
> *dusty and arid slow dying day.*

How is one to find accurate significance and meaning for the
dead when they are no more? How is one to valuate life when the
dead have taken the intimacy of a shared room with them? How is one
to comprehend the significance of one soul, when it is lost never to
remind us what great is ever again? They're leaving, leaves one *alone*.
When someone that is close to one's heart leafs, it is this *aloneness*
that one feels that brings forth new   ***meaning***.

And yet, I could not talk to her as I did before, or feel *her humility*, or her boldness when she said how she really felt regardless of what others thought; her searching kindness to calm the seas of my soul; her respect to give me *space*; her laugh though *demure* always honest, and simple. Even as the glaucoma in her eyes took up the simple brown lenses that stretched across her face, she was always delighted just to see me; her smile lit up her cracked and wrinkled face. It was a simple yet hearty big eyed smile. Nana could really appreciate a hot cup of coffee; a chocolate chip cookie…somebody to spend a little time with and play a hand of cards.

My soul touched *her soul* and she became for me a giant boulder worn smooth to my soul river's rush. What does that say about the men and women that died so many centuries ago? They've passed onto us their heritage, their lives, their losses, their triumphs of soul, and what they have endured to make out of this absurdly disorganized pig sty that we refer to as "life".

They struggled to secure for us something better, brighter, lovelier, truer, and more Godly. They passed onto us their children a piece of themselves that lies within each of us, that we should never forget, but struggle to more fully understand, until it is our turn, for others to try to understand us, and what we have to teach them. *That is our solemn duty: to learn as much as we can in our more robust seasons, so that someday, we may be deserving teachers, and with hope; die with a scrap of a dignity, that we might rightfully call our own.*

Part II.

The Womb

Meaning and Relatedness

Warm Rowing

Sometimes I get worried, *listening*; because I don't understand who is really doing the thinking. Then it appears to me still and severed, propped ubiquitously on a silver charger, "it's me who is doing the thinking. I'm just analyzing things". Ruminations morph to superfluous dynamic. "I figure I must be just analyzing things", I ponder. It's not that one shouldn't analyze, it is natural for evolutionary man to chase the logic of the noise in his head. It can at times be very beautiful… but at last, let it be *revealed* that although the sense of self within the moment may be persuading, even to oneself, at last there is a fleetingness in which this self evaporates and

> *one is again alone,*
> *humble and confused.*
> *Life is laid out*
>
> *on individual wooden blocks*
> *as sacrificial onions,*
> *bared to its knife, logic.*

Everyone is certain, and confident that their logic-chopping owes in the end to some supreme and ultimate, independent, meaningful value. Where are one's values located in time and space? It just so happens that I believe whatever it is that I presently believe, even though I may and probably will think quite differently at a later time. It is just *this immediate-felt-intimate-logic that is the eternal trickster*;

who is as if he danced
on the head of a pin,
feet pillowing
a silent levitating ballet,

dervishly revolving
as an ice performer
springing
into this imaginative void...

this metaphoric nothingness...
this absolute and unrestrained
immeasurable
containing of absurdity.

My beliefs are not my own. I am just the empty chalice consubstantial to which they fill
flavoring.

I do not own these thoughts, these *echoes of time*; however temporarily I am as if overwrought by them. The entirety of my existing-*ness* is to be held, experientially and existentially within whatever beliefs caste dominion on me, as I unaware affect their prejudices, *helplessly.*

Am I not destined to believe
that which I feel
to be the intuitive logic
of my ameliorative affections?

William James thought not that we smile because we are
happy but instead that we are happy due to the physiological reaction
of smiling. In the same spirit of dialectical paradigm reversal, have we
not convinced ourselves of the reasons for believing what it is we
wanted to believe all along? A belief glues itself to us much as the
strange oil secreted by dog shit which causes it to stick fiercely to our
sneakers, once added hard to remove.

Reluctant to change, we instead will deny, re route, distort,
and even avoid thinking entirely, just to keep the comfort we have in a
belief which emanates from another's mouth whom we have put our
filial allegiance. Another's mouth who was previously assured by
another, and by another before, and yet still another before that. Who
was it and how many generations extant before we are to arrive at the
fellow that thought as you now

believe?

We can only answer for ourselves.
We are not able to answer for others,
so if we are to search for an answer;
it must be revealed from within us.

If the basis for action is a logic, inherently flawed as
Raskolnikov reasoned to murder his landlady while at the same time
pervasive enough in its plea for veracity; then logic as a tool may be
suspect, and we mere tendrils of flawed logic's pawn. We the distilled
tangling spewed flotsam cresting the great flow, carried away all the

71

while believing it was us that is the ocean and logic our debris.

What is right action?
Ethics is a grey Sea
seething acid, jarring

the scythed membranes
of sinews twain;
skin from flesh,

platelet from corpuscle,
ligament from muscle,
soul from us,

us from ourselves
and time,
until we are no more.

Is fault to be found either in that which is one's self, or is the self somehow exonerated as one who merely mis-stepped upon the already treacherous path of logic? If logic is not immersed in ethic (existential logic), then is it logical at all? What is logic found too late, (perhaps as Raskolnikov might have looked into the mirror to see his nose loped off, his fair subconscious endeavor to spite his own face)?

Where can one bury the burden *hurt*?
How is it that one may resolve what is the *fault*,
                                    the falling off   of
their logic and its atomic avalanche of repercussions?

Joy's Buck 'kinch' saluted Sam,
 you all know those little oranges?
Just Tines quarter sliced juicy fell to.
Times own grate sluice, marked twain.
Justin Thyme, just in thy me.

It is only until another muse assumes me, then *I* will be lost, *amusingly.* Perhaps it will be the ravenous muse Hunger, to be followed by the slovenly after-Hunger muse, sleep. Curled on a coach, like a beau bowing in a womb warm, wet, rowing, comfortable and safe; I ponder, as I am known to do, the symbolic representations we call words. My lips softly caress holding the oratory sounds that grace rolling from tongue to ears, as if dancing light revealing

…"we, we'd, the womb ethic and women"
… these making love to and with a hole;
green, green, voluptuous, red haired and young.

Space is a womb, a sacred abyss
undiscriminating, undiscerning
and untouched: it is purified by humility alone.

Ancient falling echoes
through the caverns of my mind sound.
Sound.
A great echo:
Soren Kierkagaard, here's a hit for you.
I would like to be innocent.

Scarbeaus

My mind raconteurs
back into its cavern,
and a soliloquy of a girl
whose name was Michelle
in a hometown

dive of a bar
on a lonely
but commensurately
common hour
of misunderstanding.

Behind her words,
empty smiles,
made up eyes,
and lies…

(I see a ragged grungy-old-man desperately embracing a treasure that he is unable to put his hands around. His will floods rapaciously and eager, the muscles along his spine strain to bear a cargo inhuman by its un-wholeness, a superfluous un-needed bounty; (of a fallible vain man). His facial muscles contort through the make up, a disheveled dialectic, non-confluent, dis-eased and disordered by beliefs and dreams convinced they are his, desires confused, willing a feebly tattered and disoriented ignobility. Does he not know that he has grown mad, and that his madness suffocates me, this madness of agreeance, "yes's" and nods?)

Do you think that it would be scatological to contrive in your imagination a great dung beetle, perhaps the *sacred scarab Scarbaeus Sacar*, rolling along a spherical lump of decaying scat across the Nefu desert to the port of Aqaba? Her eyes try to entangle themselves in mine; I remain quiet, and look else where. But she will not leave me alone. Her teeth show themselves beneath the slip, "what's a matter?" Her words resonate at the bottom of my pipe well: "why don't you want to be happy like me, and talk and laugh, because everything is so funny hehehe".

Her apparent persistence is disconcerting and I can tell that she would much rather work on what is wrong with myself then apply a band aid to her own life. I try to look beyond the iris's and brow so furrowing, beyond the supple beauty, her complexion flawless, her breasts, lips, feminine concern, drunken stupid insensitivity; my eyes follow hers, and I try to watch her own, watching me as though she might believe she is a Saint; helping me on to a promised land of halcyon happiness.

Her long blonde curls do well to cover the shallow cast that has nestled itself charmingly beneath them. I wish I wasn't friends with her boyfriend, if I could only bring her home maybe I could get her to shut up. It's useless, if I say that nothing is bothering me, she will not believe my words. And maybe tomorrow or the next week, if we perchance see each other, it may become "how are you doing?" If I remain quiet she will persist imploring me more sympathetically, *a hounding*; "what's wrong?" If I said "nothing"; I will have given into her ground rules, and her *madness*,

so I just sit.

The thoughts in my brain simmer, as the heat from the stove simmers the stew that cooks upon it, stirring the ingredients into a consistent flavor. Maybe she is right, perhaps something is wrong. Why else would someone think? right? Either to solve a problem, because they desire to hear themselves over and over again in there own head, or simply pity. The common denominator remains the same; there must be a problem. "Why else would you favor silence over the delicacies of talking and laughing? God damn it, at least agree with me!" the troll seems to shout. *She doesn't like me to think.* One must choose either to think or to not think, to chase after thought, or not; either or, it seems there is a *leap* of faith.

West Virginia

Zen, my gato, shares with me this comfortable room in the summer heat of third floor West Virginia. I say this oven is comforting because I have not let it bother me. I have phased~back into the nocturnal schedule that allows me to read into the coolness of the night. I have refused to purchase an air-conditioner, as well, all the electricity that goes with one. The coolness of the night itself has conditioned my air, languishing with me; Dostoevsky, Sartre, Nietzsche, Hesse, Keruoac, and Alan Watts; my companions. I think I'll pour myself a drink, and perhaps, as Charles Kuralt would orate, "enjoy a moment of Zen".

My apartment is amidst a complex of interconnecting three floor buildings. From the window from which I write I can see the center Gazebo not far from me. It is a place where the old timers may congregate. Most of the people have been here for quite a while, and they generally give you a good feeling.

I watch Jackson, the run down Navy Seal who served in Vietnam start drinking in that Gazebo when I leave for school in the morning, and when I come home in the evening; he will be bombed having had nothing at all but malt liquor. Sometimes, I take it upon myself to make him a grilled cheese and bring it down to him. He says "thank you", but often can not eat the whole sandwich.

I like this, my seat by the window very much. When it is winter, I can simply put my coffee on the oversized antique heat radiator next to my chair to keep it warm. By the window there is a cricket that I saved from the maintenance men's lawnmower. I have placed him in a glass jar that had jam in it and poked holes through the saran wrap I covered it with so that he can breathe. I have named the cricket 'Friend'.

Zen sits by the window most days, and watches; his pensive form dangles from behind the curtain from where he perches. He watches the birds mostly, at night he just listens to them sing *still* by the street lights. I wonder; *will he eat Friend?*

Across from my window on the second floor lives a woman whose name is *Mary*. She is an older blond with a nice build, and a curious, mildly withdrawn yet inviting smile. She comes home around five or so. I can see her walk up the sidewalk between the colonnades from my window. Maybe I will try *to-bump-into her* later.

Zen Green

there is a soul behind that solitary shadow
in the dark that clings to the wall. A fulfillment
diametrically, motionless, curled and prehensile
disappearing beneath the curtain
 that my Mother said would add some 'character' to the apartment.

he's lonely, I wonder: does he wonder?
does he know that I love him?
do I really love him?
or do I love the idea of looking out
           ~of his skin with those vertical slits
           in his eyes and thinking how
           he must reflect upon the world?

sitting, gathering the moments
                    ….the creation and destruction of passion

the flame amongst my digits, rumbling
rubbing off the breath of life
and what of this, with his shoulders
spread wide and his palms facing

clouds, watching the shining rippled river melt with the
language, contemplative searching:

> my mind, my body, my pain
> and my love, belong to the ground;
> which has been my womb,
> but my soul belongs singularly to me

down by the crew docks
sewer water stink rolls over nipple,
lovers rumble with the crashing waves,
bodies move as if cogs in a vast machine,

ever defining creation , ever shaping the landscape,
ever ebbing love, ever flowing pain,
the two in One, the ever Oneness in Two,
molding a consumingly dominating

outline ;
a canvas
ah we are artists

> bulb beneath the shade,
> plunged a plug
> within the wall.

Luke N. Downward

Epistemology asks,
"what is a table?",
but a table
is not really a table.

A "table" is merely a word.

Gertrude Stein penned
"A rose is a rose is a rose",
but a rose
is not really a rose at all.

A "rose" is merely a word.

To these, I must ask;
"What is this word
that is a word
that is a word?"

A word is a ward watchful, confined within a ward; an award worded by a Warden in a War-den, who guards the wards in the wards, and the words in the words; the words that warn and the words that warrant, worries to the wayward wary aware, and the wayward wary unaware alike, that the words of war, are a war of words; lions roaring in dens; wares wearing wearily, utterances merrily trapped in their own wayward maze; "In the beginning, there was the word, and the word was all."

It is interesting to note that the Latin form from which English is derivative, shows that "words": **"verbom"**;

and "war": **"verbero"**, sit side by side and share the same root, "ver" from which we get *where, air*, and *'veritas'*, (truth).

If I could, for a moment ponder the greater significance of the words that seemingly rush forth fluidly images, and symbolic representations meaning other symbolic representations; each word is a mixture of utterances, non-sense or otherwise, from a voice-box, or a pen; conferring within them a proper grammar as conduit to transfer information, titles and labels mutually acknowledged conferring this authority of acknowledgement for future use and users; defined with distinction, in a tome of words, about words and their meaning based on the meaning of many other similar words… and yet where is all of this going?

So we use words, or words use us;
or
we use words and words use us;

have we not been conned?

Have we not yet been manipulated by our own manipulation; trained yet by our own tools? Could it not be the case that we are both the user of words and yet used by them as well? If words have created the substratum through which we must look at and analyze life, are we not destined solely to see through their veil?

Are individuals encouraged to question, or to just get by and "live with it"? Why should we not try to change the world so as to make people better people, smarter, more aware, more sensitive, lucid and encouraged to ask more distinctly qualitative questions? Was not the question the basis of all philosophical introspection as to the given state of things? Is not philosophy and the search for wisdom, the scientific method, and invention the basis for which we esteem to have an unfettered authority by proxy of the achievements of civilization and technological superiority leveraged by them? Why when these principles have carried us thus far should they be abandoned so haphazardly?

I hear the sounds of my mind working, the clicking of life hypothesizing various means to its end, something I am told is worth searching for and solving; however my necessary chasing entails a loss to the meaning, this means to an ending by this breathing I do; certain and fated to incline for this

death within understanding.

An orb like a house of mirrors, our head and mind is a sort of transcendental enigma whose journey through thought and life, led by an inertia of an uninterrupted obsession for chasing; as we have been resolved not to the existential loneliness of Sisyphus, but instead to the mistaken wandering-ness of the mute and uneven ball steadily heaved rolling up, then rushing through thrush, (yet only gently touched), downwards for the evolutionary gravity of the "survival of the fittest" and this   *...**nothingness**.*

We breathe, and as we breathe try to think of anything, anything at all except when one day our breath will stop. All along we are sure that it is *breathing*, and breathing alone that we are in fact doing. Breathing and living, and pretending to ourselves that living is only breathing, and that not living is not breathing and that breathing is not not-living and that not-living is not breathing.

These words cover, as a book cover covers the words, but more importantly the significance of expression; a barren sterile interpretation; a yielded scream from the pain; a soul alienated by his own master's creation of himself, as what is understood, tries to reflect upon the understanding of it; this breathing living-death, dying-life, becoming-peace, piece of expression, struggling
    …with hands down on the mat, the slovenly tentacles

of our unseen adversary wrapping themselves round our abdomen, I can feel that this ensuing struggle is imminent, and we may perhaps overtake the stealthy Gabriel for a time, but it is only to my and our demise, for as long as we are reborn to this eternally recurring moment; this right of passage, constantly evolving in inescapable *us-ness*…

And for so I think, as all along I breathe, and think of this "breathing", and deny that of "not-breathing", hysterically I search for a frame of reference, and a container for this life and my mind.

"A container", I stammer…
"I say, does anybody have a container"?
Most will reply "yes, yes here it is",
but it always manages to be

too small for my pet.
If he does not get his air,
he becomes mad.
I have heard him say

"give me not this air"
perhaps with the twitching
brown-green legs bent clicking;
I have responded "why, you must be mad?".

He climbs the rounded glass sides,
and peeks through the Saraned slits,
and looks through his lenses
at me as if to say,

"and what of you?"

Naked

Wandering into a café that surreptitiously posed as a bookshop, and even had art showings and music at times, I ogled the girl behind the counter who looked all of 25. She was an artsy blonde, attractively fit, with these super sensuous frills that came out from behind her ears. I studied her eyes, as they seemed to mirror the confidence of the intellectuals, and wanna-be's that sauntered through the nook's aisles and isles.

Dull hard wood planked floors seemed to snap to attention under-foot as women walked bearing down on them with their high heels, a-rhythmic but accenting with panache the cool tones of jazz the room breathed. I wondered if this artsy blonde was just part of the mystique of the place. I looked toward the window, out gazing at the mid afternoons causeway confusion and disorder and felt elated at the calm which presently surrounded myself.

There was a seat left by the window, but not facing it, facing inwards with a small round table. It looked comfortable, black and leather. As she turned around I had a look at her buttocks. It was nice and skinny for a girl that age. I ordered my coffee, and brought it and the Egyptian 'Book of the Dead' with me to the window seat. What would I do with myself with all the time I would have if I conquered what has most ailed me, that which separates how I know myself to be presently, and when I was younger, happier, and more certain?

And though all may be lost,
the jazz still plays
and I am still here.

Somehow, when some things are uttered, it doesn't much matter as to the nature of the resolution that they are spoken in. They are nevertheless misunderstood, and inevitably so is the person who bears their fruit. The moment of departure, these words spoken, can not be retrieved, yet without them something false exists *in the*

85

relation. Timeless are the strivings, for a piece of time, that merits an understanding of what has happened and that which holds one somehow *justified*, if in only the fact that they had done, what they had thought, and felt it best for them to do.

> *The bare creation*
> *out of nothingness,*
> *and it's nakedness to others.*
> *Time makes man weak.*
>
> *The moment to moment,*
> *within the womb ethic…*
> *bleeds a living color,*
> *a solemn yearning*
>
> *undying warmth,*
> *a just love, and a kind*
> *appreciation which*
> *does not assume.*

When I say words like "*appreciation*", it is how I grasp the word that I mean to convey. When *echoes* utter words such as "*appreciation*" while within the *womb ethic*, the words spoken becomes askew and aslant to misunderstanding.

The word feels *different…* somehow *more real, more tangible*; because it is experienced and explored more completely and maturely. When I convey this meaning within meanings; when the other side of my skin reckons forth through spoiled spoken word, it is with fool-hearty frivolity and a clear lack of patience at that which I may never master, but instead must be at last resigned as a petty peddler, piddling pedantically the 'blossomy ornament'. *My meaning is lost and I within it.*

I stood flat-footed in a shower, water-sheet grained and grazed, filth steam razed rained upon my face; calmly brow burrowed I studied the echoes heard between my ears while in the womb ethic. I studied my *relation* to others… when in the womb ethic, and not. While in the womb ethic, stillness asserts, "why act?" the past is fine; my relation to myself and others orbits around this *is-ness already*. On the other hand, if I were not in the womb ethic, the calling is "why not act?", then the future and what I am to become, in essence my drive is the shaping force in my various relations.

The *is-ness* is determined on what I create, what I become; so it is that my mind naturally works to strive and prepare for the future. In the womb ethic, it is exactly this preparation for the future, this other minded-ness, and the need for preparation that feels hostile and breeds anxiety. I would like, in the womb ethic, nothing better than to not prepare at all but simply to understand what is going on currently. But most of us must confront the necessity of preparation. We may choose either to abort it, and thought itself, which is essentially useful, or face the fears, and the ethic of thought, and other minded-ness; the duplicity within life, that of is-ness already: the fact that the past brings with it meaning existentially; and also that of becoming: that we are continually obligated to create anew through action.

Aleister Crowley said "do as thou wilt; thus is the extent of the law". But it just can not be. Our choosing is dependent on the values that are actualized dialectically, as meaning itself is experienced. Within "do as thou wilt" there is an abdication of *will* rather then *value*. Gone from this is Kant's necessary inconsequential argument to "do the thing which you deem to be an end-in-itself". Value must be created experientially as one must reach back into the historical annals of time to see how one's values must relate to those current and those dead.

Intelligence does not exist in a vacuum but is instead filtered through an existing-ness; which must firstly always be forced to choose and to act; thus it must be that this is a determining factor on one's intelligence. If one is not ethical, then they are not intelligent, no matter how clever the display. The burning question that should be in everyone's soul is precisely that of ethics;

"what should I do? what is right action?"

But man is not always able, if but rarely, in rare extenuating circumstances, to ask himself thusly. It is only within the womb ethic that he gets this chance to

"sit and make progress in this"   ~Lao Tzu, Tao Te Ching.

Thoughts of the past, the present,
and the possibilities merge into one;
one ethic; Oneself,
and there is at last a peace,

an understanding;
a rest and a breadth of time,
and there is an appreciation for it.
"Ahhhhh....life", I sigh,
"and birds chirping with it".

Heavy Water

"If the government is anarchic
the people are honest.

If the government is meddlesome
The state is lacking", ~Lao Tzu, Tao Te Ching

If only I could reach into my belly,
and turn my stomach inside out,
so that it may be empty.

When it is full
I am unable to bear witness
to my own emptiness.

Yet it is necessary to gaze
into your emptiness.
I should go hungry.

The ceramic Mexican tiles intuit
the shaky-ness of the flesh
 which treads upon them.

My feet falter, staggeringly,
unsure; my dry toes screech
and I stumble forward
in the dark. I reach out with:

obscured fingertips,
my proverbial fancy sticks,
and ancient eyes.

The automatic dishwasher changes cycles,

"kerplunk".

When I was a child,
the giants among me were like red woods
to my youth and inexperience.
As my roots took hold,
my own branches grew strong,
as they instead grew still older,
greyer,
shrinking it seems

down; there is only so much time, yet we
are never able to grasp how much, or even if we could;

how much this time would mean.

The days go by, faster, and when the light goes out, we are
once again reminded of our time. When I was young, *Time* was like a
piece of sweet candy, but I knew all along it was a queer despot.
Mostly, I saw regrets in the people around me; that and my Father was
very stoic about dying. "Everybody's got to die", he'd say.

> *But "die" to me,*
> *was to leave,*
> *and never come back.*

My sister Marina taught to me about:

astral projection, and the Bible;
Heaven and Hell;
as well as Jesus Christ
and Satan.

> My Father on the other hand,
> talked about the World Wars;
> about General Patton and Adolf Hitler;
> and about the League of Nations,
> NATO and the Warsaw Pact.

There was an epic theme within these conversations, the spirit battles of ancient lore and those of our mechanized Modern age; that of good battling evil. When I saw the video clips showing the atrocities that happened within the gates of the Nazi concentration camps:

of the bodies shot collapsing in mass graves,
of the flailing limbs lifelessly piled by inertia, bulldozed and helpless,
the incendiary rubble and grey ash,
the gas chambers and how the victims watched their families
collapse as smoke from stacks which rose as Moloch untamed,
the images of the people behind the barbed wire,
faces and hopes and identities collapsed inward

within the images and eyes drawn poor of walking skeletons
from behind the guarding ghetto wire;
> it effected me at the level of my soul.

I couldn't understand why, or how somebody could willingly
hurt so many people, so callously, so utterly without remorse. *How
could somebody do this*? my burden breathed forth. But what I was
really asking was: *"what is evil"?* Yet to understand what evil is: is to
understand being evil. "How could someone do this?" At first I tried
to think about the victims, and to imagine the existential grasping they
had to do when their life was up, but it seemed so shallow a judgment.
I could not possibly imagine what it would be like to suffer such
injustices. How can a mere man become a cruel monster? The
question was like a fever that consumed me. And so I took to
imagining what it would be like to do the things Hitler and the Nazi's
had done. This was not immediately neither easy nor attractive but I
imagined that it was I who was murdering the Jews, helping to escort
them into the chambers, on and off the rails, even cutting their hair
before the "desensitization" process with the foreknowledge that they
would be killed; shooting those too helpless to defend themselves, and
even their babies before them. I tried to imagine, but I couldn't step
inside, to see who that person was that was dying. The sheer numbers
themselves became unreal,

how is an individual who is murdered become a number?

a 1 in 11,000,000 ones?

To even try to grasp the magnitude of the crime was itself
EXHAUSTING. Yet I placed the responsibility of understanding upon
myself; this epic undertaking of empathetic hemorrhaging ... maybe it
was the images of all the emaciated prisoners within the camps that

distressed me; standing there unkempt and filthy, fingers clinging desperately to the fence haunted, looking outward

... with those their eyes...

Didn't I in my search for self knowledge owe to them the consideration for what it means to be treated as one-who-is-like-others and yet different enough to be considered lower then dung? Who else would remember these alienated souls thrown as ashes into an ash heap and spread over? Who else would even consider

... a number naked?

The eyes looked directly out of souls and into the rolling cameras which held their images barren as deserts, so timelessly; knowing full well that any attempt to communicate to another the unfathomable events that they're eyes had witnessed, would at last be impossible.

Yet their eyes spoke... so I tried to imagine the life of one boy, of a similar age to myself; of being ripped away from one's childhood, one's comfort, games, friends and future, to be forced into a ghetto like an animal is a cage, to watch your parents and siblings shot before you, to be filed into the gas chamber, *followed all the while by eyes for whom you were already dead,* to be made

just a small part;
of teeth, or hair,
or a senseless pile of bones
that the Nazi's stored sadistically in rooms, to be made into:

soap or stew

… to be utterly negated as an empathetic and sentient worthwhile individual. I could feel him, feel inside him like I was him, *losing*

…then I imagined killing this boy I had created in my mind, *this me* thrown into the Zeitgeist of the 1930's, and with the killing of *this barren number*, the killing of all the other *numbers. It was then that somehow,*

the numbers became   ***real*,**

each a soul whose eyes looked outward
beyond the fences that held them before me;
helpless herded chattel, good for nothing
besides the allowance of misery
that they were allotted before their deaths.

What evil must exist in the mind of one who is unable to appreciate a single one soul, to wish to destroy that which he could not appreciate? What evil must exist within the soul of one who would destroy an entire people? What ignorance must exist in a people who do not understand what evil is, who choose a tyrant before their freedom, who passively or otherwise participate in the slaughter of 11 million helpless people whom they lived next door to; whom they bought bread from; from whom they borrowed sugar, with whose children their own children played… how out of control stupidity can befall a people, how swayed and utterly controlled by propaganda we can become. How resistant to thought must we be in choosing in our own mind *the values that we will live by…*

One has either to accept the Holocaust as an abomination against humanity or condone and absolve it of any true value judgment. To one who accepts the Holocaust as morally repugnant there are essentially 2 things that one must learn from the Holocaust: that the Holocaust represents the purest source of evil known in human history and everything that happened in the Holocaust was essentially "legal" according to German Parliamentary government record; in as such the principle to be learned is that:

being lawful does not equate with being ethical.

As such the Holocaust serves as an exploratory pedagogy: for if one were placed into the same circumstances would or should one do that which is *ethical* or that which is *lawful* if such a time presents itself where the two do not meet as if in simple confluence? How much stronger would one need be first to be able to realize beyond the illusion of mob mentality and again the courage at last to pull away from the mob and to accomplish the *ethical act* with no hope at all of reward or even acknowledgement?

Yet *how many* people on this day will take the time out of their busy schedules to reflect on the life of *one* soul who died to become merely a number, partially because of our own willed stupidity?
How many?

11 million is just a number, and far too large to even grasp or comprehend. It *feels* much the same as *1 million*,
or 100,000,

or even *20,000, it seems.*

The number and the people subsumed within the number become insignificant, and somehow lose relevance. A hundred people one can put their arms around, mourn, reflect and feel empathy for. What is the meaning of 11 million people being slaughtered like cattle purposefully and without shame? Yet 11 million is not even one life, but a mere number in a void. So many lives, so hopelessly lost. And somehow it seems to me that each of these persons deserves their own number alone and a part from the rest. Each single line, a single 1 which could so emptily represent them instead of the mass grave and fumes which held their deaths so meaninglessly, a number of their own, a line to represent our loss of them, a single line so that they may have in death what they were essentially denied in life; the right to be treated as an individual… this is *with dignity.*

Place a 1 next to another 1 next to a another 1, again and again without skipping lines or spaces, for 367 pages, at the number 12 font. Print this up, hold it in your hands, and then realize that each one of these 1's was a single human being. Each single line represents someone who had a biography, and a family; thoughts, fears, desires and just a small moment on this earth like us all to bloom; but their lives were stolen from them during the Holocaust; and understand again, *how ignorant a people we must truly be in order to let our own brothers do this to each other.* The first thought that comes to one in trying to comprehend how 11 million people are destroyed is inimically Biblical, "they must have done something, right?", otherwise how could there be both justice, and at the same time no justice at all? Of course the people can no longer defend themselves against such a charge, because they are no longer here… the Nazi's punished them solely for the cruel enjoyment of their masters;

destroying not only
their lives, but their bodies,
their souls, their will,
their God, their hope, their trust;
and with all this,
any evidence at all that they even existed,
and perhaps for the far greater part,
even our very collective memory of them.
Power itself in the minds of most
who would not wonder
has become the ultimate ethic.

I looked onto the cloth textured walls and the dark oil rubbed
wood floors of my Mother's ornate living room, and stared at the dark
night colored panes of glass that stretched to the top of the cathedral
ceiling and the 40 years that had passed since the end of World War II
and

it: time

seemed so distant

and so cold.

I was in rage; how could anyone fail to understand these
people were alive *once, "and you ruined everything every one of these*
people had. These .....were real people. How could you do this?" I
shouted from the insides of my soul out to ethereal fabric of the evil. I
realized that I had felt this evil such that I felt I knew it intimately.
Within the squalid air of inner recesses stored, hiding from ourselves
the us that we don't want to know of; I could feel this evil so close,
perhaps because in my imagination I had served to carry out the acts I
held so detestable... and there before them I stood screaming down to
the dark and pitted bloody evil red.

"Ahhhhhhhhhhh! Evil! How could you?" I remember being so angry at Hitler. I knew he was with the Devil because that's where he must be, and I wanted to soul fight him, and challenge all the evil. It frightened me, but I thought if someone was brave enough to fight the evil, to challenge it, and if they were of pure enough heart, that they could somehow destroy it, because in the end evil must be weak, and good however poor, fortified in strength.

Epistemic Legos

What is the basis for epistemic knowledge? How is it that we can claim to know something and how is the very way that we perceive life related to our sensory perception? The ear is an 'analytic' organ (it picks things apart), while the eye is a 'synthetic' organ (which instead blends things together). The eye synthesizes (green and red) so that it sees things as one (brown). It says *"this is it"*. One may discover the ear only by:

> *depriving synthetic perception*
> *and closing ones eyes.*

The ear exhibits more humility, in that when it hears, it hears the mystery (something of which it does not claim knowledge of). In a piece of music it can distinguish between the different instruments and pick them apart (analyze them), unlike the eye. Remove language, labels, and symbols as such and you might hear the ear muttering *"what is it?"* The ear conquers with feminine passivity like radar; by enveloping it understands the shape of things and as such can exhibit its control with more finesse.

The ear is the more primordially phylogenic sensory perception of the two. Since evolution's introduction of the eye, organisms have become more reliant on it, and its inherent structural reality; and conversely less reliant on the blinded radar of the ear and its antithetical structure of reality. Hence we see a movement in myth descending from plurality to oneness, pagan gods to a monotheistic One; from many more humble reasons to explain cosmology, gravity, the earth and action, to one *"this is it"*.

It goes by many names of which 'Science' is one, 'Logic' another; which conversely to the ear, operates out of phallic urgency, penetrating in a rather pushy and insensitive way to get to the essence of things and can by the way of this black/white essentialism control by limiting the boundaries of the dangers as such and acting in a way to progressively limit, compartmentalize, label and understand by way of continual re-classifying along continuums of difference. It is the purpose of evolutionary man to delineate the factors which might contribute to a dangerous turn of events; the dangers of chaos, of grey, *of the ocean which is ethics and our lives*, the Sea of value, and how the *relation of words and meaning disintegrates* upon closer inspection. It is this that evolutionary man has evolved specifically for.

According to Buddhism, we suffer because of our "attachment" to things. In order to be free from Samsara and the karmic cycle of suffering, we must therefore *un-attach ourselves*. Un-attachment it seems here is the goal but can a human being in action ever be completely non-attached? If one is a disciple of non-attachment, are they not therefore still attached? How is one to be not attached to, and to what?

The illusion?

The Buddha's idea that "all is an illusion" must have an epistemological reference point. *That which holds that "all is illusion"; must too be illusional*, being itself a part of everything that makes up this over-arching illusion.

In the lotus, during meditation, with eyes closed, the Buddha could hear things; and by hearing them, *hear them*, as a radar reads the sounds so as not to simply cast aspersions as to the appearance of the thing, but instead honed, surrounding and enveloping the thing, giving it its space in time, *alone*; and by not seeing and attributing what the cause of the sound was;

magick happened.

He was lost first in the sounds, and then to the question that comes when one does not automatically label that which they hear, "*what is it*"?, his soul seemed to breath clear. His ears would not add things up the same way that is eyes would, to pronounce "*this is it*". He could only listen, to the different sounds, be they birds or his breath or the humming electricity like-buzzing which came from nature herself; and he knew he had found the unidentifiable energy of *magick,* again in the life that realized its own life *first*.

He recognized it from childhood, maybe lying in the grass fresh with dew, or perhaps watching the ripples forming in a pond. It was what he was searching for his whole life. *It was not that everything was illusion, but more specifically and importantly that the basis for the valuation of the sensory-epistemology of the ear and what it tells us about this life and our self is qualitatively more significant in its puerile humility, than the sensory-epistemology of the more sophisticated lawyerly eye. Life is not "this is it", but first "what is it?"*

> *"Between 'yes sir' and 'certainly not'*
> *how much difference is there to be had?*
> *Between beauty and ugliness,*
> *How great is the distinction?"*

> *"How nebulous!*
> *   as the ocean;*
> *How blurred!*
> *   as though without boundary."*
> *   ~ Lao Tzu, Tao Te Ching*

Within the qualities we find in music lie both their greatest attributes as well as their greatest flaws. The seminal and preeminent act of which I speak of is its tautological namesake: "harmony". It is the proposition that there can be an overarching theme, a unity to music and therefore as existentially experienced, a unity to life. We are temporarily comforted within the sense of harmony. It seems to say to us; *"there is meaning, there is some sense to it all"*.

The meaning is wrapped up and contained within harmony. What this hopeful idiocy would desire to negate is the inherent power of the dialectic; that *{by being increased one is decreased; where there is unity, there is chaos}*.

Chaos is the dialectical antithesis to its poor brother Harmony. Musically, the best example of Chaos that I know of can be found in *Miles Davis' "Live at the Fillmore"*. Chaos *is* it's unity, the answer to the question burning inside the heart of every living soul whose pain resides in an ever penetrating ache that refuses to find solace in the Harmony of music, in the harmony that tells you to keep quiet as it smothers your breath with the pillow whispering discretely that it will take care of everything.

Epistemically speaking

The Berg of Konig was a short stocky little fellow, an eccentric enigma, a scholar of impeccable credentials and a true man of thought. Immanuel Kant forthrightly wrestled with empiricist epistemology in his time, spoke of 'noumena' and 'phenomena', of one's duty, universal laws and the very possibility of knowledge as something which happens between the thing-in-itself as it is unblemished by our perception of it and secondly, our marred perception of it. With deference to Heisenberg and his principle, there must first be addressed the issue of interpretation:

thought itself is an object of which not the individual but only other thought may have access to directly.

M*aybe there is no knowledge* between the mind's reception and that which is the subject of thought. *Maybe there is just a relation*, between that which appears in the

> *mind, and in the heart,*
> *and it's relationship to everything,*
> *and nothing that can be said;*
>
> *to the Indian drums beating,*
> *by the fire in the night;*
> *to that which praises that which is sacred,*
> *and is appreciated as sacred;*
>
> *to man's relationship to his destiny,*
> *to meaning, to communion,*
> *to courage, and to his death.*
> *Otherwise how would one establish the*
> *knowledge of thought as an object?*

Thought is in essence an object, and the essence of, would be in Kantian terms the 'noumena'; how besides through other thought (which is thinking and using other thought to opine on the First thought divorced from it many times over) would one have access to their own thought? Man does not possess his own thoughts, (that he is

103

not consubstantial to his thoughts), therefore these thoughts are not truly his, but instead, barren naked echoes just passing through, (kind of like us).

What I mean to say is that if one has a 'first thought' (lets call it), and we would like to understand what this first thought is or an interpretation would be, we do not have direct access to this first thought. We instead must access it by using other thought indeed to conceptualize the first thought within the various contexts to which it is to be made useful or serve as a means to an end, etc. etc. Through various uncontrollable variables including but not limited to mood, time of month, stress, hunger, other concerns (more pressing or trivial), age, etc. our thoughts are played and replayed, extracted and modified inside our brain.

In short what would thought be in relation to?
Thought must be relation's own reflexive
understanding of its own relatedness;
but this would be madness.

The moment passes,
the time fades,
dies like me;

the feelings in the moments pass,
die, morph into different moments,
until it is that I die.

To think that there were a million years before today; even a billion, and that there will be a billion years after today; makes me feel like a very small part, of a very small moment in time, yet extremely privileged, to be alive in the miracle of life; to be alive in this moment of history, not in human history, but in life history. May nobody think of the lives of the dinosaurs or any number of extinct species; of a single bird, or even a worm that may have witnessed the Sun rolling down, and what a time this life is, as much as we now can, and do. Like so much of them we will vanish as dust on the plain, and

in the plains in the heart of our own marred relatedness.

Warble Wobble Round Retro

Is God Depressed? And if not, why is empathy
so synonymous with a deep felt sense of loss?;
that feeling of connection, a desire to stay there in that
... nothing?

And yet somehow we press forward past the earlier tribal stages of reclusive, hermetic, transcendental spiritualism; because we must procreate and as well provide and prepare for the arrival of the generation to be. God striped of all grammatical capitalizations, statuesque idols, myth, liturgy, and rituals… the deepest sense of a being is the *stillness*, the chastity of ego that one achieves in self knowledge where the illusions around one have crumbled.

If perchance I am not already an asshole, could life convert me yet into one? Would it matter if others agreed that I am an asshole, if I was not one in-deed? What would matter more, what they thought, what I thought, or if there was a truth: that truth? What truth? Kierkagaards? Socrates? They died. They met their end… What is that end to which we all go, floating ever towards? (Do some die worse than others, or do we all depart in similar fashion)?

> *"Decrease and again decrease,*
> *until you reach nonaction.*
> *Through nonaction,*
> *No action is left undone"*,
>
> ~Lao Tzu, Tao Te Ching

So up is down, and down is up and all that, so there is nothing: perhaps pain itself, or the absence of it could not even be used to be the sole discriminating factor in comparing the death of one to the death of another. If not pain, then what could, or would be used for such discrimination? the damnation of one man's soul? of a womb man's?

> *"The tyrant does not die the natural death.*
> *This I take to be my mentor"*
>
> ~Lao Tzu, Tao Te Ching

Has this modern technological age ruined our own immortality, by stealing from us the *God-within-us*? Is there not a much deeper link to which religions have assimilated the essential socio-biological elements which are the foundation for civilization proper and the basis for the ethical decisions made therein? Our new God: the Scientific Method, has replaced the cosmological soothsayers, and destroyed with it a way-of-relating that was *essential* to our species.

> *"Nothing under heaven is softer or weaker*
> *than water and yet nothing better for attacking*
> *what is hard and strong, because of its mutability"*
> ~ *Lao Tzu, Tao Te Ching*

Evolution is strong like water, mutable and therefore resilient, but is it possible for a species to *regress* by artificially manipulating the environment so as to change the way it relates-to-itself? Could we already be in the process of such an evolutionary regression, and if so how would we know?

If all the humans on earth as well as most of the animals died on the planet and all that there existed were the alligators and a few other remote species, just enough for the alligators to get along, and if we could look down in spirit upon this place after we died in the physical sense; would we look upon these scattered and bewildered beings and claim them as our own, in the hope that there could eventually be something else; something to create the works of Nietzsche again, the personality of Christ; and the transcendental enactment of life looking back at itself?

Would we at last relate to those still existing cockroaches as cousins-in-life? Would we see the need for progress at all, or would we like the simplicity and deadness of everything? We could create this deadness, us together. We could blow up the world, and call the alligators our own, or not call them our own, but today at least, we could be cognizant to the comparative reality of it and could call them our own.

Did God weep when Martin Luther King was murdered? Did Martin Luther King weep for his people when his own end befell him? Was his death a tragedy and would or could he have reconciled this with a belief in life after death? Did his mouth drop wide open in awe of the realness of his death revealed pen-ultimately before him? Would he have regretted the crusade he had led to free a people and a nation had he known the end it would bring to him? How would he have reconciled this being an ethical choice if he understood by foreknowledge that there was no afterlife and no salvation?

Where along the continuum of quotients would he have rated the regret or stupidity he would have felt towards what he had done with his life had he known that the Christian God of the Old Testament was merely a depiction and an amalgamated admixture of the Egyptian Book of the Dead and complex ancient Astrological studies of the Zodiac?

Could he possibly have been more proud to fight for something, which had not verifiability in any absolute sense, but a value system that he had if not created, than participated in, and revealed to deeper and more meaningful depths both existentially lived, and experientially defined, courageously undertaken, and themselves radical examples of what it means to be an ethical man?

The Shinto belief system that guided the Japanese Kamikaze pilots of WWII, didn't allow for life after death, however they were willing, (or not so willing when they'd give them just enough gas for the one way trip), to die for an abstract idea, or their family, or their neighbors. How would they ever know that the reason that they were dying counted toward the attainment of some end in a war long lost?

Would it matter if it did… in the last 5 or 10 seconds before their plane burst into the target, what about the last 2 or 3 seconds, when he could see clearly the different colored brothers whose lives on the deck of the cruiser he would end? … At the last moment?

> *What courage of perception*
> *must it be to see death*
> *and the void of nothingness before you*
>
> *to look into it, and again away…*
> *to watch the last of a life*
> *that you have known go by?*

Crazy Dust Frazzled

Still, I in the *dark, lay* quiet in *my bed, and listen.* My mind *chases* the textured contours and *intricacies of survival,* 'Are the *doors all locked*? Yes I think I *locked* them. I should go check, but I already *checked*. Someone could always *come through* the basement and I would *hear* very little. Maybe I could rest more easily if I *got a dog* that would be able to *hear* all of the *sounds* that I am unable to. What was that noise? It's as if I'm *hearing* short beeps *frazzled* through the ether, but it can't be because I'm in the woods.

I lay *stiller* still, and listen for anyone … *moving*. If I'm completely *still* and my *eyeglasses* are off the pillow, (so I can't hear the *flickering* of my *eyelashes* against the *cloth)*, then I will surely hear something if it *moves*. I hold my *breath*, but I can't hear anything. If I were breaking in I'd be listening for another who audibly heard the break-in. If they were smart they would try to listen to me listening, otherwise they would not know if waiting around the corner for them with a cartoon sized frying pan ("doink") was someone *who was* listening. It has very little to do with who is a better man, but instead it is all about who is there first and who retains the element of surprise; thought is like a sewer pipe laid along the outside of a pyramid , 'shit rolls down hill'. It is necessary for those who work in the shadows to retain the element of secrecy, for invisibility itself is their power.

Hmmm…. Is it that my 'Neptune is in Uranus' or that my 'Mercury is in Retrograde', so to speak, as I attempt in frivolous fashion to collect and undermine those beliefs within the history of my life as I have told them to myself. Was it *my imagination* alone that propelled me to believe that my cohorted peers of my early childhood attempted to expunge me into the solitary class of the social-outcaste? Can I rely on the corroborating evidence of others in my memory that saw the same as I?

When that wrangled gesticulation of a child "Kenny" would try daily to torment my existence was it really as I had told myself 'good battling evil', or did I enjoy this fiction of mine; of being the representation of good, and of being chased by a self created fiction of evil? I suppose I was a clever enough child …was Kenny the representative of unrestrained malicious peril or was he just a kid without a Father around to protect him, trying to make sense of it? Yet here I am, still huddled under 4 blankets, too cheap to turn the heat on, holding my breath and listening for intruders, all the while worrying that they might be watching me through the windows.

What are the chances that I could lose my life or that I would be unable to defend my family against an intruder? A nightmarish horror film might outline the scenarios a bit more distinctly; *our only chance at survival lay that we out-think the problem, define the boundaries of that which we deem to be dangerous, and defend ourselves.* The Horror film delineates how sometimes when we wake up, the nightmare does not end. It is right that we should be prepared for just such an occurrence, because as History teaches us, they do happen. Consider the Holocaust; the evil exhibited within the Holocaust is inherently paradoxical; the ape at layers within each of us, primordial, violent, controlling, and dangerous was unmasked, unfettered, and released into a darkness which aligned itself

with death smoking.

Am I alone in the fact that I do not trust the system to keep me alive? It's a rather large wager, and irrevocable as such. If one is right than they live another day; however the day that they are wrong the cost of the wager is life. *One must continually redefine the boundaries of what they deem to be dangerous if they are to protect themselves and their family.*

Obviously fewer murders happen in the suburbs, still, a more accurate predictor for behavior would be a specific town; for instance 'Douglas' so named from a Scottish battle which left the river red, *'Dub Glas'* meaning: 'blood river'; how many times did a house get broken into and the culprit killed someone in Douglas last year? … I can't think of one; so either it did not happen or no one found out, or I just didn't get the e-mail. Over the last 20 years, how many murders happened in Douglas? None to my reassured knowledge, so 20 years times 365.25 days is 0 for 7305 days straight.

I must be as sure as I can be about something in order to go further. *How is one to go on, to choose again, if what in their mind is not made clear already? How is one to choose out of an ocean, what right action is? When they solved the mystery of how values relate to our own meaning of them?* **What does meaning mean**? *Are we not here with this last question at a dead stop? For if we do not have an answer for "what does meaning mean?", than are we not just talking in a round about way about nothing?*

Maybe if I wanted "the meaning of meaning" I could look it up in a dictionary, right? I open the dictionary to the right paragraph, and it portends symbols but does not explain to me what the meaning of meaning is. The meaning of meaning is not found in a book of symbols. It is like the question; *"what is the value of value?"* It is because these things seem obvious that we have a working knowledge of them and can ignore them and treat such words and questions as meaningless drivel.

It almost seems as if to me a Goliath in a doorway which I must pass. It is ironic that others may never come to this portal, or hope to graze its threshold.

What is philosophy without a meaning of meaning?

How can we even talk through symbols without such a meaning? it must be obvious that we don't need such a meaning for it is I who is still talking, using meaning, and you who are still reading or listening. Let's see what it says in the dictionary again; *duh, I confused.* in the Oxford dictionary and Thesaurus American Edition the "meaning" of "meaning" is

1). what is meant by a word
2). significance
3). importance.

The first meaning is a tautology and offers us nothing so I'll have to rely on the others for help. Why is it "important"? Wouldn't whatever would make it important make it important by what it meant, if what was meant was really important? What is important anyway? to us? to God? to us if there exists a God? Couldn't God really have the final word even if he does not exist, having changed one's life, and the society's relational value judgments as an existing idea alone?

What is my word worth, more or less? Is there such a thing as "more or less" in relation to meaning between man and God? What about between me and God, is that different, or must I always think of myself in terms of other human beings? Is that all I am, a human being? Isn't the word "human being" inconsequential? Even what it *signifies*, just a theory, that we are a species, and not a dream in the mind of God, isn't that too *inconsequential*?

Well it might depend on my level of seriousness or yours if I admit you exist. I'm writing not you. Has this nest a meaning inherent? a one hand clapping?; the discarded ladder in Wittgenstein's Tractatus: *"where of one cannot speak, one must keep silent"*? What about for a single cell paramecium? Does the OED establish the meaning of meaning for him? I'm sure that such an understanding of "one hand clapping", (if that is in fact an understanding), would elucidate for him this simple question, (is it a simple question? a question upon the universe?).

Does my life make more or less *significance* than a single cell paramecium? Just because I thought so would not make it certainly fact, nor would, if I said not. But I am talking and making statements for only a small part of the universe it seems to me; possibly just my universe. My universe? Lol. It does not exist. *I'd say that "I exist" however it is really only that which becomes me.*

Does meaning go beyond this threshold?; or is this the end all? But even so, only for a short while; the human species will be obliterated in a blink of universal time, for the most part inconsequentially. In life, there is space and time, and nothing else may exist forever. And out of all this, how could I have the audacity to say "I exist"? Before today, there were a billion-billion trillion yesterdays that I knew not, nor knew me, and after this day yet a trillion trillon billion tomorrows yet to be, yet without me. If one were to start with the Universe instead of their own selves, they would see that in the grand scheme of things we don't really exist. The appearance of our existence is real to us because it is *happening* and we become part of this happening as we are immersed within it; to the top we float as a blanket of pond scum, transitory, microscopic bacteria and insignificant filth.

We actually think something we say or do has meaning? We are the dust of the universe, its dead fallen skin; times flagellation, spaces temporal annex. I wonder if God has ever felt the same way, and if he has, then no blasphemer am I. *Blasphemer am I?* ... I've made God in my image, as Moses has before me, as he wanted others to believe in Him, so he made God. I am entitled to the same, as I dust too, am eyeball to this universe, a fly on its wall, and that is it. I postulate that:

$$M = C(ST)2$$

Meaning equals choice multiplied by space/time, (squared for the exponentiality of chaos). The meaning of meaning is: *that I dig.* That's what I do, like I'd like to dig into some Canadian bacon in a bit because I'm hungry. Mmm... Canadian bacon tastes even better as I taste it and think that it is a dead pig, because I remember again that I am alive, and forgetful of this.

What does it mean to be alive; to exist? Does it not mean to die? Ever the difference must be felt, if the moment is to be known as what it is... and what we are...

transitory specks of dust,
the universes dead fallen skin.
It's opiatic to consider such things but again;
the difference:
when I am not thinking such things
what is important?
The civil war?
Digging the foundation?
History or brushing my teeth
before listening for intruders
anxiously under covers?
Anxious dust.
  Crazy anxious dust.

    If the dust of us were as crazy as the dust of me, how
different would we all see the universe? that is if we cogitated it as
such. Yet we are alike, no dust I can understand, for I am like to the
cycle of the universe, as dust is to my own cyclical home
maintenance; Definition #2, of no significance, definition #3 of no
importance, *hence meaningless.*

    At this point what is ethics?

        and what is right action?

            as a human being,
            as a being,
            as I,
            or as the dust?

If I am meaningless,
then what is meaning?
Surely there must be meaning
if there is meaningless-ness,
for meaninglessness implies
the negation of meaning
and thereby admits of its existence.

Meaning must be our relation
to that nothing that we are all in;
and part of the Space/Time,
that is unimportant to all,
but most important to all.

That which we never think of,
sustains us,
outlives us,
is beyond us,
 with us;
is us,
but not us,
has and dispenses meaning,
meaninglessness, lies, truth,
good, evil, significance

... and *nothing*.

"Clay is molded to make a pot,
but it is the space where there is
nothing that the usefulness of the clay pot lies",
~ Lao Tzu, Tao Te Ching.

Roles rolled and rolling roads around

In the end, I'm *caught in it*, as a fly stuck sticky in a web worn and cunning. When I ask myself what I should write, is it not the same as asking of life exactly: "*what has value*?" "What is truly worth doing?" But in the search for ethics, (~the 'study of what is right action'; i.e. the meaning of my singular quest to understand life through my relation to and with it); what is presumed is that if one analyzes enough the answer will become revealed to them, (i.e. that there is in fact an answer and it is achievable).

C.S. Pierce said that we think in order to reach a belief, to appease the irritation of doubt. Still, thinking arrives at false beliefs, though they might be comforting ones to be sure.

What is belief, and what more importantly is doubt other than the belief that yet other thought or fear is worth chasing after in one's mind? In reflection, we are in the end left alone with our moments, as I am with you here as if a buzzing-stillness captured alive and seen through these Saraned slits revered.

Is belief merely a comforting delusion? Do we have beliefs or do beliefs simply occupy our being temporarily; as if possessed by a thought disease?
I lose course of action.
There is no reason for action,

and I have no reason to resume course of action. But alas, it is this thing called life that I have witnessed and that is happening before me that appears as etched blue ink scratches on thin slices of grained wood timber, and that has presented itself consubstantial to my being.

but the children are outside playing,
thoughts of coffee,

the young girl refereeing
'downed with light brown hair',
running now,

more thoughts of her   (oh stop it!).

Here's the question: time is experienced
as you spend it with people. *Time is*
as you learn about life, *through* people.

In ways, I feel I've become part of the people
that I've known and had the occasion
 to spend the most time with.

... suggested intermission for the Beatles...
"the long and winding road"

...blue ink momentum
life is: waiting to die...
therefore:
life is death waiting

"the maitre'd morte;
let's see Da'ath, who will you have?
yes, you will have all,
all but one, and that is Life".

Life has won over death, we live, or else I did live (maybe if
someone reads this, probably I am no more; 1= 0, ha)..

If life had not won over nothing,
* I could not pen these words.*
What is death's relation to life?
to be no more,
?
or
that which never was
never again will be
?

Must we be relegated to the meaning of that which can be communicated, of that which passes through the sieve of language? Is not what can-never-be-uttered at least equally as important in the *quest for meaning*? If what is not, and can not be said is equally important as what can be said, and people must content themselves in understanding each other; and therefore themselves through the narrow *prism* of what can be said; then what have we?

> *The self is just a theory of a thought,*
> *thought a theory of an echo,*
> *heard but not bottled,*
> *never distilled*
> *nor ever owned.*
> *This paper is but an ornament of life.*

Even I, as my mind chases to collect, and fails to connect; even after all I chase, I chase still; therefore I chase to no purpose. "Chase. Do it"; my mind implores me regardless; "chase... *chase, why*"? But I with others is different *somehow... let us eat breakfast and come back...*

I can't believe I am (knock on wood), healthy right now. I breathe easy. I have a woman and child, and a mortgage, and a job. I am with the people, the people that die. I too will be nothing, someday.

Someday I = dust.

I hope flowers like me, or birds or animals,
someone...
I hope someone enjoys me.

I've enjoyed so many; pigs and chickens,
and cattle, and fish. I've taken many apples,
I've roasted many trees, peanut butter sandwiches,
coffee, blue ink, all comes from somewhere,
something, some other's labor, some other's labor lost,
someone else, some other that is = no more.

Forsaken are the chickens that have nourished us without
even the thought for a life that is no more. Their parts come
compartmentalized as naked numbers dismembered, cut, packaged
and frozen for our ease; and yet, we have no blood on our hands, only
ketchup, and mustard stains our clothes.

"decrease and decrease again",   ~*Lao Tzu, Tao Te Ching*

How am I to look at death? For this I have no answer. Yet, it
is the deepest point at question particularly because it determines how
I will look at life. I again come to the point where I say "I am alive",
yet others are dead. I say "Yes, but the people who are with me here,
and those whom have not yet passed away are *still* with me". Yet I say
some of these "alive" may yet be dead; I just have not heard yet,
                    … I do not know,

and yet... I say again I have been with those "still with us"
before they ... died, yet they died too; *still…* I am stunned; what is
memory's relation to death? Aren't these that died of high importance?
Yet why do I have such paucity of memory? One carries a piece of
another with them and becomes one with another *who either is no
more; or who experiences a revealing of a different order.*

We must as surveyors always traverse back from prior coordinates to more fully understand where we are, where we are going, and the nature of the dialectical reverberations that are happening within us. Here is an ethical enigma as I see it; if one's meaning emanates from all that is meaningful, and this includes past meaning from those that have died, as they were; a those who do not make their meaning seen; how does one balance and properly interpret the import one should give to those who have passed, differentiated from those walking

still with us?

Where is the import divided between the life found in books and that found outside your window? How should one separate and define *the sacred difference between what is ethical and what is in accordance with the law, however unethical…* or to intuit and serve with justice the boundary? How could one communicate what a trip their life will lead them to a child? Misunderstanding is a foundational trait of man.

And the sign above the entrance of Auschwitz, the largest mass extermination site in the Jewish Shoah, which we refer to as the Holocaust read *"Work brings Freedom"*. What is it that the secret silence of the language unknown reads to the fair feathered flock gutted and quartered for their mis-fated sweet taste? Is it perhaps: *"barbeque sauce will set you free"*?

Question words.
Question every single thing.
Question today and *today*
determine that you will question more tomorrow
because sometimes it is within the question itself
that the answer may be revealed.

And at last I am just a man or a speck of dust. A temporary
flickering, like the prismed-wings that carry the scarab; I too am the
fruit of this life. We have a time on this great Earth, and that is all. To
what place we have in this time we may never know, *but we do have a
time*, however small, to flower. Let us then flower, for it is all we may
know, *until we are at last One*. When we are not thankful for some
end to dedicate our lives to, then we are neglectful of *our most divine
role*:

>   *to appreciate*
>   this life that is before us
>   and to treat with significance
>   the humility that meaning breathes…
>   Life gives so much,
>
>   if we cannot give back,
>   if all we ever do is take,
>   then it is forever taking itself
>   that takes, and takes from us:
>   **ourselves**; *thank you, I'll sit.*

But this is at last   *shit! Hand pressed,*
patted, formed and   *forged, rolled rolling*
and laid... Alas, out of   *this earthen womb*
`   *crawl thee out and fly as yet*
         the primeval ones   *have*
          never yet   *flown.*

            Be
           marred,

            be
           born

           and
          become

Meaning and Relatedness

Beadle Scat

Meaning and Relatedness

Beadle Scat

Poems on the Path

By Khepri Rising

2nd Edition 2010

Cover Photo of Beadle Scat, First Edition

Meaning and Relatedness

Poem Index

Meaning and Relatedness

Beadle Scat

In deep appreciation for
a Love that once saved me
and a girl whose name is
forever Trisha Jean,

may I ever rise to kiss your soul...

Meaning and Relatedness

Beadle Scat

Meaning and Relatedness

I.

Time Twained

Joy's Buck 'kinch' saluted Sam,
 you all know those little oranges?
Just Tines quarter sliced juicy fell to.
Times own grate sluice, marked twain.
Justin Thyme, Justin Thyme.

Meaning and Relatedness

Bang

Energy is goodness
within appreciation
which is still.
Startled by consciousness
of matter which awoke.

Light bled forth
by a stillness darkened.
Goodness is not Nothing,
but something within nothing.
Goodness collapsed small to a point

like a bodhisattva might sit soft on a grain;
how ~ intuit and love
imploded into that One
until it was almost *nothing*,
so immense and

so *still* it seemed everything;
without seams at all.
Goodness seeking/
not seeking = stillness.
There still

in the sacred darkness,
our universe sheered forth
as like *an epileptic seizure*:
vibrating beyond itself,
claims and what it knew itself to be,

birthed true, new,
and at the moment of explosion
when it was destroyed,
it became a new;
what is always had been

a yearning known not,
the knots kneaded, heated and undone
 much as a point,
collapsing unto itself,
and thereby destroying what was the self,

like a shaman to become…
so undefined as
appreciating stillness
 explored and unafraid and
still with what is;

then fire;
something then nothing.
By ascetic gravity,
it created all,
we are what is left

of its matter seized.
Matter is energy that is good,
appreciating and still...
To be still is to have no limbs,
and no head at all,

to cut away everything,
except the heart.
It is to not be at all,
And as the heart
is the river to our body,

so God is the river to our being,
so are we riding
a river back to God,
Tiny incandescent stillness,
energy, collapsed to the point:

we are not that which is,
but that which flows,
Lao Tzu was close to God,
he was like a river,
washed upon our shores,

God-like,
he touched us,
showing us how selfless love is,
how stillness flows,
and if we are to be God-like,

or experience our Father,
then we too must be like
the very heart of the river,
we must at last feel ourselves
as this perilous *flowing rush.*

II.

Lotus Blue

An old blue kite string
and ribbon saunters guiding
the clear water running

as it presses gently over
rocks smooth to the wear,
feeding into the nurturing

mellow wet valley of the lotus.
The lotus is made warm
by the yellow Sun on high;

laid cool by the darkened
muddy mottled waters
on low. The two spin fast

like a children's fan
breath blown;
it is that child

who may see through…
The petals of the lotus
are the smooth, soft,

fruit dressed for the dance.
The colors of the trees
freed fallen float

amongst the season's
last chance prance.
Left in the sift,

a deft silt drift;
it leaves and cleaves
to the mottled

muddy leaves so
that some day
when the time

conceives, they
may again give life
to the lotus.

Ethics

What is right action?
Ethics is a grey Sea
seething acid, jarring

the scythed membranes
of sinews twain;
skin from flesh,

platelet from corpuscle,
ligament from muscle,
soul from us,

us from ourselves
and time,
until we are no more.

Meaning and Relatedness

III.

Zero

There is no mass.
There is only the individual.
Individuals may conspire,
but they are individuals none the less.

Any attempt at grouping
must remain at best: abstract,
a creation in philosophy,
at best a creation in utility.

In order to live within
this reality one might have
to become like Gandhi;
an outcaste by choice.

He was an outcaste to abstraction,
but not to the people.
The problem begins in childhood
 identification through groups.

The individual achieves the status
of being "one of" the group.
 "Us" and "Them" is created.
And then "Us" is lost.

And there is just "I" and "Them".
It is then that we submit to the
million year old ritual of marriage,
creating the next "Us" and the new "Them".

Could it be cognitively based?
Could man and woman have evolved
to become not only the more mate-able,
but better companions?

If one were not to find a mate,
a universal inclusion in "us",
one is banished from the gene
pool and from all of eternity.
Following a life of frustration,
depression, despair, and possibly suicide.
Marriage is a 'marring',
a destruction of the self.

Beadle Scat

But meaning must continue
to be made at the most elemental
and individual level. One
must in the end, separate.

Claim nothing. No identification.
No religion. No political party.
No fashion. No nothing, but everything.
Nothing in particular. No-thing.

There is no mass,
therefore no reason
to dominate an abstract mass
which does not exist.

There exists no mass to dominate.
There is no mass to fear.
One is not "Them";
one is himself, or herself.
Why fear an individual?
There is no reason.
There is no reason for anxiousness.
There is no code.

Code does not exist.
All that exists is what
we create. What we can create
amongst individuals is

an end to the madness.
But in order to do so
we must first be 'beings',
apart from the madness,

apart from the chaos,
and awake.
Nothing exists.

Clean

Empty cogitation chasing
bird shit on sill sitting
before me as I in
my solemn wooden chair ache.

What if life had been different?
the burly drops of rain
show their wares
wearing heavy on my sill shit.

Grey skies donning
make the morning mist
reveric in its solitary confinement
And so I am led around

as my mind chases,
chasing my mind chasing...
this life:
what more could I have done?

Meaning and Relatedness

IV.

without title

Thy woes bellow forth foes,
whose leaves these are that blows,
a Thee's which is amongst me;

A sea that is before,
beneath, and encircling me.
Mar marring Martians

and Martins and Martyrs
and Maries and marrying
Marion marionettes.

Who is this that is,
who envelopes me,
develops and transcends me,

who I become,
who absconds with
everything that I am not,

who loathes even
 that which I am?;
who is but an echo,

something heard after,
and that is all?
And all is us:

and one may
sit by a glass,
and wonder

how our star died,
and blew up
before it was supposed to.

Why make pictures
about appreciating life,
when in the end

there will be not even that?
There will be no reason,
there will be nothing.
And far be it a shame
in my heart, the burden
a branding in the soul of man,

Beadle Scat

our evil is ourselves,
and I guess life itself:
man collapses by gravity

unto himself like a star,
implodes.
Satan has his art it seems,

and yet...

there is so much good

and yet...

after when all we know
is no more ,if it did not matter
or if it did matter,
and it doesn't matter
and it does matter,
that there will be something

or nothing at all,

everything and nothing
that we can imagine

that we are no more,

no more heartbeats
within the universe,
 if it is a uni-verse,

what will this energy be,
will it be feeling or thinking
or growing, expanding,

 collapsing, if it is but a
mere cytoplastic infinitesimal
blurb within the heart of it;

 "what is", if there could
be such a thing,
 if it could be communicated,

or even barely conceptualized?
Is it the heart; everything?
Is that why meaning

                    is in everything?

Is that why we are anxious,

and don't understand...?
Is that why life is so confusing...?

Is anything worth
 paying attention to?
Is anything worth doing?

Lao Tzu said "one should sit
and make progress in this",
still sitting is doing,

but it is also
hearing and listening
and wondering

and listening
and listening to the listening
 to listening

till it glistens
like a singular single
alone, undefined unmeasured

unlabeled un-purposeful
bent prismed shining light

captured yet dancing

        as a perfect drop   floating

seemingly
on nothing
 but the barren raped perceptions

in my mind;
 no fears,
no tears

       un-maimed yet marred
       eternal yet vulnerable
       indestructibly falling

       and curving still,
       still-ly morphing
       as if fluxed in a river flowing

         so that it has: no memory;

nor any words at all,
the tempest before words,
the drop before the tempest,

and before the drop,
dropped from the heavens
it was rounding,

and rolling
and bending
and swerving and free;

the drop was free.
The drop was me.
And the drop is

still my perception,
still as I see,
still as I imagined

to ever will,
breathe, bear
and be.

Meaning and Relatedness

Zen Green

there is a soul behind that solitary shadow

in the dark that clings to the wall. A fulfillment

diametrically, motionless, curled and prehensile

disappearing beneath the curtain

 that my Mother said would add some 'character' to the apartment.

he's lonely, I wonder: does he wonder?

does he know that I love him?

do I really love him?

or do I love the idea of looking out

    ~of his skin with those vertical slits

    in his eyes and thinking how

    he must reflect upon the world?

sitting, gathering the moments

    ....the creation and destruction of passion

the flame amongst my digits, rumbling

rubbing off the breath of life

and what of this, with his shoulders

spread wide and his palms facing

clouds, watching the shining rippled river melt with the

language, contemplative searching:

my mind, my body, my pain
and my love, belong to the ground
but my soul belongs to me

down by the crew docks
sewer water stink rolls over nipple,
lovers rumble with the crashing waves,
bodies move as if cogs in a vast machine,

ever defining creation , ever shaping the landscape,
ever ebbing love, ever flowing pain,
the two in One, the ever Oneness in Two,
molding a consumingly dominating

                         outline ;

                         a canvas

                         ahh we are artists

bulb beneath the shade,
   plunged a plug
    within the wall

V.

5/5 and wind-tripped

cavernous ripples march wind swept
through sun gold, light blue and navy rays divine;
the soul is a sutured chasm that must
hold fast to a vision
that the self within one knows to be true

the flight of a bird
has no words
as words themselves,
arise then float inexplicably,
and from where they emanate
I know not other than their floating

Later...
they did not see that
I was once a child too
a child through
and through
I did not know
that it is the truth of
his voice that I now seek
when I feel empty.

Meaning and Relatedness

Smoke Float

The moment *passes*, the time fades,

morphs and blends to create

new *passing-dying-time*.

Fear is a thought disease.

Feel sorry for *sorry*,

but sorry only,

for nothing is sorry but sorry.

      Anything else can be determined

      by everything, anything, *nothing*…

      and nothing I can say…   …

      Their thoughts, pause

                 floating

 in mid-air, … then are no more.

New thoughts and old thoughts; *float*.

As the *seaweed* slime drags

the dark moist brown sand,

slithering as only a liquid blanket *might*,

and chasing to catch up to its *waves*

… *it waves*.

It could be an *assertion*, true or false,
a *question* plausible or hypothetical,
appropriate or lewd,
asked honestly
or clandestine with foreknowledge;
perhaps a statement *of* semantics
or an allegation *founded* or bogus;

it could be *an* acclamation of some *selfless*
service performed, banal, extravagant or *unique*,
or perhaps a *conviction* of some moral crime
deemed inexcusable by the mass *or* a mass,
or any particular applicable propagandas
judged to be:
'motive-for-interest',
as or belonging to the Church of Law,
or the Church of the modern-day-assholes,
made in good faith, or perjured; or ultimately
to be taken within any of the other plausible
and exculpatory methods to be deemed inclusive
with and adjusted to the nature of that
which we may rightly term the: *war of words*;

Even thusly : must it *float, then perish forever.*
Only I am here. Only I am here, *untouched.*
You or I or they may think.
But no one may *touch* me with their thoughts.
I can not be thought. They can think.
But that is it. *They can not think me.*

Meaning and Relatedness

Provident Dub Glas

On an asphalt laden path
that rises up
in the scattered
earthen ruins

of a cemetery
and grassy knolls
to end in a place named
for divine Providence.

Mar rushing Blood River
pipes beneath SeaMain
Road,
runs smooth

then empties
into the thickets
 betwixt the living,
 and the sullen,
greying, lonely,
 stolen stones,

and wet wind blown
brown grasses stir;

streaming, screaming,
Suns beaming,
light morning
cold hazy air,

sounds of passing
automobiles, and
hot air
leaving the valves;

the Jake-brakes engage,
rattle-thump/hum
some gurgling before the turn,
the turning up route 16,

as we in our stream
screened past
in luke,
 lovely- lowly-laying
 lying-ness;

a gushing, with
 flowing changing-ness,
and a becoming
swerving-ness
again, until it enters
the pipes beneath
the poles of '4-1' and '4-2'
which I take to mean

"for one... life",
(as 2 and B are
 inextricably related),
and exiting boldly

as the river
marred
into the Womb Ethic;
WE: our pond;

Me: a pawn,
I am forever there,
and there…
forever a time.

We'd

…"we, we'd, the womb ethic and women"

… these making love to and with a hole;

green, green, voluptuous, red haired and young.

Ancient falling echoes

through the caverns of my mind sound.

Sound.

A great echo: Soren Kierkagaard, here's a hit for you.

I would like to be innocent.

MAR

"But mirth is marred, and good cheer is lost"~ Dryden.

"To Mar": as in "tomorrow",
a frame of convenience and a creation of ambiguity;
a place where one may divide for the sake of meaning
and ritual what will never again be,
and what must yet become;
like a martyr murdered and marred,
a mirage rat-trapped in a mirror's razor.

Hence we have:
marren: "to hinder or obstruct"
and mers: "to trouble or confuse"
at its root it is "a blemish" or a "disfiguring mark"
and yet it is the indefinable;

like the God Posiedon,
in Spanish and Latin it is: "the sea",
and as such; dangerous and unpredictable,
wrecking havoc as "a virgin mother" might

frame   or   signal
the   end   as   well
as   the   beginning.

For the 6 million years preceding the last century
man has evolved a mating ritual which involved
the structure of safety that fatherhood
and the family afforded to their children;
a protection and guidance that other species
could not have had the benefit of because they
did not evolve the mutation of "cryptic ovulation".
Humans did, and how like out of the grey matter
of the wolf the many species of dogs evolved,
we too came from a grey undefined
and dangerous as the Sea of marriage.

When a woman failed to show when she was fertile,
when she herself became non cognizant
* as to her reproductive faculties,*
sex and access to her became valuable,
and for this man evolved to trade things for it,
and womb~man evolved to sense what it was in a man
who would value this in her enough to stay
and value what became of her, and their children.
Men traded more and more,
until they traded themselves for this,

and essentially became no more,
but one of two twain into destiny,
a bare naked moment in man's evolutionary history.

So men battled with each other for access to womb~men,
and womb~men battled with each other
for access to the dominant men.
It would be rather simple to say that bartering was born,
it would be a bit more accurate me~thinks to say
that personality itself was birthed.

Man knew woman, and woman knew man;
and they continued to know each other,
because there was no other way
for the man to be content
that the children he fed were his,
and no other way for the woman to know
that the children she had would be fed, and cared for.

Sex became valued for itself, and man became crazy for it;
because those that were not crazy for it
failed to find as many vehicles for their genes
as those who were more addicted.
And women learned to use
'what they got' to manipulate men,
because those that didn't learn

didn't pass on their genes nearly as much
as those that did.

And so we have the species valuation of "virginity",
and the necessity of shotgun weddings.
When two were "married", they were destroyed
and born anew unto each other and their children.
When they picked each other their families assured
through custom that they would be expected to fulfill
the roles as was expected of each other.

The man provided to a woman his resourcefulness,
and woman brought to man
her inherent ability to bear his children.
It worked nicely for the first 6 to 9 million years
of human evolution.

From it we gained an infrastructure
which allowed us the safety to develop,
to travel, to invent and manipulate our environment,
to create and use fire to warm ourselves,
to fuse a nearly prehensile finger
which mimics our own highly
adaptable and resourceful nature.

Beadle Scat

As our cousin the gorilla grew large enough
to beat off his brothers from
what would become his reproductive destiny,
he grew larger and larger as in their mating
structured habitat allowed, as it is natural
only the largest and meanest gorillas
furthered their genes; as the chimpanzee
grew not large, but instead large testicles
to produce as much sperm as his body would allow,
and the more sperm he produced
the better chance that his seeds flowered
and not his big-balled brother
who slept with their cousin just before him.

So the human too evolved not large, but large brained:
his own tool for evolutionary success,
the tool which would allow him to win over his competitors
by either being more resourceful,
or being able to deceive another
that he is more resourceful,
and all the variants along the continuum in between.

Marriage~ Marred
What becomes of a species that has evolved along
a certain path for some millions of years,
but then through the occurrence of some feature
which artificially or otherwise changes the way   the species
inter- relates to each other:
what happens when marriage itself is marred?

A generation or two ago a man and women
went to church to be married,
today they go to a court.

A generation or two ago a man and woman heard rites
from a robed priest or pontiff on a pulpit in a ritual
which had evolved and survived over millions of years,
to bind and make them one and surrender unto each other
their lives and their souls;
today instead they arrive at the Church of Law,
to be unbound; "marriage" itself is "marred".

A generation or two ago a couple stayed together
for the "sake of the children",
today they part for the good of themselves,
women 80%, men 20%.
A generation or two ago a grandmother might say
to her granddaughter:

Beadle Scat

"why buy the cow when you can get the milk for free?";
tomorrow they will say:
"why keep an old cow
when you can get his milk sent my mail anyway?"

A generation or two ago if a man had a child
with a women he would be expected to marry her;
when my child was born our fathers shook hands
and hers said to mine:
"well you know the chances that these things work out
aren't that good",
they don't need to be apparently.

A generation or two ago a man kneeled to a women
to ask her hand, opened doors, and had time with the kids,
today he is either a "dead-beat" or a visitor,
neither a father unless they are a lawyer
or "connected" to the system that parasitizes
and destroys children's families for their "best interest"
much as the money changers were in the church
in Jesus' day, today they are in our families,
and the church of law today,
insidiously profiting from the abuse
of other peoples families, without conscience.

A generation or two ago a married couple
could not get divorced until they proved fault;
then beginning in 1970 the divorce lawyers
and their agents of ruin by subterfuge
snuck in a no-fault divorce law
and sold it to a nation as an improvement
and even greater freedom,
even though the only two other times this abortion
reared its ugly head happened when masters of people:
the Bolsheviks, and White American slave masters
decided that their subjects did not deserve to have
their families protected so sundering their children
from the evolutionary protection of having two parents.

A generation or two ago the people
who really run this world,
the media and what we are told got a little scared
about the African American community doing pretty well,
and thinking for themselves,
and standing up for their rights
and having a leader with golden balls from heaven
and of a pure heart unsurpassed;

and so they killed him,
and gave him a day and laughed
and killed the President,

and gave a half dollar,
then his brother Robert who loved them;
and then when the country had the lowest degree
of poverty in its history,
the Presidents successor from Texas
where John F was murdered
began his "war on poverty",
and the first thing he did
was to expand the benefits for mothers
who kicked their husbands
and the fathers of their children out of the home,
and knocked on the doors of their houses like a plague,
to made sure no father was present
before they gave the check.

A generation or two ago the front organizations
for secret operations and secret operatives
and other organizations that go by the name of "philanthropic",
funded by the families
who really run this world, gave money to an
educated class of women who were discontented,
bitter, and angry at men; perhaps justifiably,
to catalyze a movement that would spread
distrust and a lack of faith,
and what would come to be known
as it was given credence by the people

that we see in the circus on TV
 and the circus in print media,
who nodded their head in accents,
and thereby directly gave sanction to a new paradigm
and an unmitigated disaster in societal bigotry
 focused as a laser on all men,
but especially those on the lower stratum of economy
to call all men" rapists" and spearheading a movement
that would hurtfully stigmatize and demonize all fathers
and begin to defraud a man and a woman
of their own children without even their knowledge of it,
by giving the power of their children's lives
over to strangers whom they have never met
and later the lead movement that would be
the true killer of the civil rights reform
for the benefit of all people unfairly suppressed
by simply turning half the population
against the other half.

And black women's attention away from the actions
of the people who kept them down
and sent their children to schools that wouldn't teach,
but instead to find solace against their husbands.
They played a shell game, and as we watched the magician move
from civil rights to feminism we couldn't see that they were just
turning us against ourselves.

The keys to freedom not had they won,
only the restraints of stronger shackles.

A generation or two ago
the people that really run this world,
 used the Vietnam War to sway attention away
from the secret war and the bane seeds
of a domestic holocaust that would tear apart more families than
did either Hitler or Stalin,
and used a bullshit story
that we landed on the moon
and we watched those desert astronauts
spear a flag through a colorless sand, planned,
and as we watched it wave we thought there had to be a reason
that it was, even though we knew
that there was no wind on the moon,
because there isn't any atmosphere,
and so we believed we landed on the moon
much as we would think of Santa racing across the sky
to slide through our chimney,
and eat our cookies and milk.

But Santa brought presents wrapped with bows,
and the people on the moon brought us pride and wonder, and
social security would be our safety net,
and the family courts could be trusted because whatever they

did, we could be assured, that it would all be
"in the best interest of the child".

Just a generation ago Archie Bunker
steadfast and honest, granted a little bit racist,
but even the black people laughed then
whenever Jefferson went to Archie's house;
Archie and Jefferson were two real men
that captivated us, with their comic failings
or their exalted glee, stubborn, hardened,
and hard working, but always a men,
Why is it today that the men they parade out as real life are
either hen- pecked bitches or caricatures,
If tough then dumb, perhaps aggressive yet lacking empathy or
balance, and too often, humility;
or they split your side with laughter
but remain effectively effeminate by submission,
or endure a prolonged self aggrandizing adolescence.

And now there are shows about shows about shows,
And actors playing news men
and sometimes the President,
we hound the stars with flashing lights of cameras,
at their homes in their bathrooms,
following them down the road
to see who they are fucking now,

wherever they go, shamelessly;
we ourselves pay these cultural mercenaries
much as the government claims we support terrorism
by smoking a joint to our heads,
we pay for the animal cruelty of our own race
by watching the programs that support this kind of racket,
and we watch how people's lives are destroyed
but we never hear the media question
that perhaps they are taking part in the downward spiral of
those that are not quite as narcissistically adjusted at being a
public spectacle; and the somehow these retarded sheople that
follow and follow and never think,
nod their heads as to sanction the mistreatment
of their of species, and laugh in amusement,
it is a wonder to me that this is legal
whilst cock fighting is illegal
when they are doing essentially the same exact thing;
and the sheople mock their responsibility when they assert that
these people "agreed" to this
simply by becoming more famous then themselves,
swallowing the bitter pill of schadenfreude.

and so it is that perhaps tomorrow
we ourselves, as a society will more easily
nod and give sanction, to our own lost freedom,
when the others have framed us in their monitor,

the fate justly earned by the sheople who bleat,
and bleat only, the bleat of their neighbor, the bleat of their
family, the bleat and the "skeet skeet skeet" of a movie or a
singer or some other shithead, the bleat which is the blight
forever virus upon their children unaware.
We have become the feeble caricatures of a dead species, a
rotted species, manipulated by laws and lawyers and assholes;
we've become dogs dead to our own natural selection, selected
instead by a process of animal husbandry similar to that which
dogs are bred.

No longer does a man have a right to his family,
to see his children, to his role as guardian
 and father and control his destiny and resources;
these are but play fodder for assholes in yachts
who rule the world and the very minds of the people
whom they have led to believe that they are free.

A generation or two ago men and women were married,
today we live in a mirage and an amalgamation
of what life used to be like,
and the shit hole it has become;
and the only way that they can continue to sell it
 is to make us dumber and dumber and dumber;
"Are you smarter than a fifth grader?"
between the Hollywood stars being chased around,

and the stories of the "successful people"
that they would like to project on TV sitcoms,
the lawyers and the doctors shows that depict
 how some people are so successful,
all the while the middle class
has been shipped across the seas never to return again,
 nor America, nor humanity.

And does humanity or ethics or dignity
even matter anymore when the great majority
resolve their issues and discontent with
pharmaceutically engineered designer lifestyles.
Really why would a man strive to become
all that a man could be,
if all he had to do is simply pop a pill
and chill out to the cool propaganda?
And the great lie told by all to all,
that smoke stacks is for them and their children,
and not us and ours,
until our hair is shorn we will not believe,
and we will not see.

First they threw the black fathers out of their homes,
And we nodded our heads,
then the white fathers were taken from their families,
but not so much the lawyers and the doctors

and the others who profit, so they say nothing

because they believe that their children are safe,

but probably you, as you read this,

and you're own children

are in grave grave danger,

and you do nothing.

A generation or two ago we were married,

whilst today we are marred; our ethic and us

came from the womb encrypted and cryptic,

and it is there that we must let again

 *reveal unto us: **ourselves**.*

Beadle Scat

Beadle Scat

Meaning and Relatedness

About the author:

Khepri Rising earned his Bachelor of Arts in Philosophy/Religion, and Psychology. He is also the author of Baptism of Fire (2010) and Cipher-Dios, (2011). I humbly thank you for reading my book. I spent 13 years on it and feel very strongly that I was directed in ways that I cannot comprehend by a force of light which I am unable to explain. I practice no religion devoutly, but I aspire to someday follow the words of the philosopher or teachings that I have come to admire the most, those of the Chinese sage LaoTzu.

Email Address:

Rising@Howling.com

Meaning and Relatedness

<u>Inspirations and Considerations of Gratitude:</u>
Lao Tzu, Buddha,
Moses, Bob Marley,
Alan Watts, Nietzsche,
Gandhi, Dostoevsky,
Professor Newman,
Hemingway, Kerouac,
Amiri Baraka, T.S. Eliot,
James Joyce, Joseph Campbell,
Martin Buber, Nancy Rappa,
Professor Plumley, Professor Yeager,
Professor Campbell, Professor Yake,
Professor Curry, Sartre,
Hesse, Wilfred Owen,
David Jones, Thoreau,
Kant, Aldous Huxley,
Professor Madigan, Oakleaf,
Buz, Joe, my 3 K B's,
and *Trisha*.

Meaning and Relatedness

Beadle Scat

Meaning and Relatedness

Other books by Khepri Rising:

~ III. Baptism of Fire 2010

The Holocaust within the Family Court Industrial Complex and Post Traumatic Family Court Disorder, (PTFCD)

~ IV. Cipher-Dios 2011

The Historical Quest into the meta-labyrinthine mythos beneath Star Wars, the Gnostic psalms of our time

~ V. Aten Gleams 2011

Poems of Disintegration

Part 1 of the Marah 2012

The Becoming of Dinstinctive Meaning

Meaning and Relatedness

Beadle Scat

Meaning and Relatedness

Meaning and Relatedness

Beadle Scat